OUTLAW COUNTRY

A Western Adventure

A.T. BUTLER

CHAPTER ONE

Jacob Payne, a bounty hunter in the Arizona Territory, heard the altercation in the crowded saloon before he saw it.

He crossed the threshold of the Golden Saddle Saloon and let his eyes adjust to the dim light. On the right side of the room, nearest where he walked in, the bar was packed with men elbowing each other for space. A half dozen of Holly Merritt's girls squeezed in between, entertaining their guests and helping them drink all the beer that the bartender could serve. The bright colors on the women stood out against the dirty leather of the men, and Jacob smiled to himself to think about how each one of those women would be happy to take their money.

It was a Saturday, and it seemed as though every person in Tucson was in the saloon trying to fit in as much sinning as possible before the Lord's day the following morning. Past the bar, tables throughout the room were crowded with men playing poker, drinking, grabbing at passing women, laughing, and telling stories.

But on the far side of the room, back where the gamblers Lucky and Abe had virtually been living for the last couple weeks as they took all the other men's money, a shoving match had broken out.

"I'll show you—" an angry voice called above the noise.

Jacob pushed through the crowd to get to the skirmish before it could spread. His broad shoulders and more than six feet of height made him a formidable force; men saw him coming and got out of the way fast. In a few purposeful strides, he had reached the brawling gamblers. He hesitated, and in that split second a short and stocky but fit red-headed man Jacob didn't recognize landed a punch right to Lucky's cheekbone.

"You son of a—" Abe yelled as he pushed the short man back.

Jacob stepped between them and put his hands up to ward off the gambler. Despite the shorter man's powerful hit, two on one would never be a fair fight.

"Hold on here," Jacob said.

"What's all this?" a deep, gravelly voice asked angrily.

Randall Hall, the owner of the saloon, glared at Jacob. "You causing trouble in my establishment, Payne?"

Randall stood to his full height. Though several inches shorter than Jacob, Randall's wide barrel chest asserted his authority. Holly Merritt waited just behind him, her warm brown curls piled atop her head and a gold shawl pulled tightly around her. She surveyed the damage to the saloon with an anxious look.

"No, sir," Jacob answered patiently.

Before he could explain any further, the short man Jacob had intended to protect knocked into him from behind as he made to go after Lucky again.

"Hey!" Jacob stumbled aside.

The unknown red-headed man threw himself at the gambler, pummeling him in the ribs with punch after punch.

"That's enough," Randall said, grabbing for the shorter man.

Jacob regained his footing and again stepped between the brawlers. This time, with Randall's help to hold the one back, they succeeded in ending the fight.

"What's this all about?" Randall asked, his voice low and severe. He glared down at the man in his grip. "Mr. Timson, I would never have thought a man of your profession and class could be involved in a common barroom fistfight."

"What did you boys do to him?" Jacob asked the gamblers.

"Nothing," Lucky said indignantly, shaking off Jacob's grip.

The bounty hunter was almost inclined to believe him, seeing as that denial was literally the only word he had heard the man say in the several weeks he had been in Tucson.

"You did, you—you—cheating snake," Timson spluttered. He writhed in Randall's grasp, trying and failing to break free from the man almost twice his weight.

"Is that true?" Jacob asked.

Lucky glared at him, but Abe held Jacob's gaze. The gambler spit a long stream into a nearby spittoon before answering with a sly smile.

"We simply used our considerable skill at cards to relieve this man of some of his paper. Really, we're doing him a favor. Less weight to move when he inevitably leaves town." The gambler grinned mockingly at Timson, wide enough that Jacob noticed for the first time that the man had a gold tooth on one side.

Jacob shook his head and sighed. "Come on, Abe. We both know what you're capable of. Did you cheat?"

Jacob's eyes darted over the man, looking for a sign he was hiding cards, but saw nothing out of place. He glanced to the table, where the cards were still strewn about after the last hand. He raked over the edge of the poker table, and even underneath, looking for a mirror or any other clue.

Lucky and Abe had been playing in Tucson for weeks, and though they had been accused of cheating many times, none of the other men had been able to prove it. Jacob was beginning to think they really were just extremely talented players.

As he looked over the men, he noticed the crowd that had gathered to watch. Most of the saloon's patrons had lost interest once the fight had been broken up, but two men continued to look on. The taller of the two—taller than Jacob but thin as a rail—leaned against the back wall, biting the nails on his filthy left hand and pushing back his stringy dark hair as he took in the scene. The other, a blond, was as average-looking a man as Jacob had ever seen, but wore distinctive moss-green cowboy boots. His face remained passive, and he hovered just behind Holly while he listened. Jacob had never seen these two strangers before; at least a dozen questions and suspicions popped into his mind. He filed all these details away, just in case, but forced himself to stay focused on the situation at hand.

"I can't have any more disturbances in here, boys," Holly said with a teasing lilt. "Ruins the mood, you know."

She caught Jacob watching her and winked. Though he had never personally been a customer of Holly's, they had always had an easy repartee. He respected the way she ran her business, and she respected the way he did his own work.

Timson's chest still heaved as he caught his breath. His anger seemed to be abating. "Just give me back my money, fellas, and we'll forget all about this."

"Not a chance," Abe said.

Instead of responding with words, Lucky simply glared and walked away. He pushed through the crowded saloon and Jacob lost sight of him.

Randall moved to follow, but Timson stopped him.

"Let him go. It's this other one that actually has the cash. I saw him scoop it up when I first pushed his friend. Whatever it is they're doing, they're in this together. I just want my money."

Timson reached into his coat pocket and pulled out his billfold. Jacob couldn't help but notice it had a small red rose embroidered in the corner of the leather. He had never seen another billfold like it, either here in the territory or back when he lived in Virginia.

"You're not from around here, are you?" he asked.

Timson looked at him in surprise and shook his head. "No. Just passing through. I come from Boston, by way of about three dozen smaller cities between there and here."

Before he could explain any further, the conversation was interrupted yet again by a familiar voice.

"Jacob Payne, why do I always find you in the middle of trouble?"

Jacob grinned and greeted Deputy Tobias Lowry with a warm handshake. "Trouble seems to find me, sir."

"Don't I know it," the deputy said pointedly. "Is there anything the matter here, Mr. Hall?"

Randall looked from Abe to Timson and back again, weighing his next words. Jacob didn't envy him this position. The former had been a paying guest in the apartments above for weeks; the latter just arrived but seemed to be spending just as much money, and even faster.

"I think we may have just had ourselves a misunderstanding, Deputy," he said finally.

"But—" Timson began.

Randall put his hand up to stop the protest. "Mr. Timson here may have just paid for a very expensive poker lesson, but I'm sure he won't make the same mistake again."

Jacob was surprised to hear Timson growl under his breath, what with a deputy now present. But then, it was usually the shorter men who had the most fight in them.

"I'm not going to stand for this," Timson said. "Do you know who I am? I'm leaving on the first train out of here."

Jacob cleared his throat. "Sir, Tucson isn't on any rail yet. Didn't you notice when you got to town?"

"What? But— Goddammit!"

"I'm sure you can hire a stagecoach, though. On Monday. Or—"

"Never mind," Timson said with a huff. He glared at Abe, Randall, and Jacob all in turn before turning his back on them and disappearing into the crowd that had all turned at the sound of his yelling.

"That's a shame," Holly said lightly. "I was counting on his business for another week or so at least."

Randall shook his head. "I'll go try to talk some sense into him."

With Timson gone and no longer making a fuss, the watching crowd dispersed, including the two strangers Jacob had noticed.

"Did you see what happened, Jacob?" Deputy Lowry asked under his breath.

Jacob shook his head. "They were already fighting when I got here. Lucky was the one taking the punches, actually, but I didn't see anything out of the ordinary. What do you think, Holly?"

The woman shrugged daintily. "Those boys have been here every night, have managed to irritate most of the men in town, and yet no one can pin anything on them. I'm inclined to believe they're just better at what they do."

"It is *all* they do, after all," the deputy agreed. "Well, Miss Merritt. I'm sorry you're losing that income this week, but it's probably for the best."

She nodded. "I'm sure you're right. I'll go

see if I can smooth the man's ruffled feathers." She grinned at Jacob and flashed a dimple. "You boys behave, now."

Once they were alone, Deputy Lowry chuckled. "Trouble really does seem to find you, doesn't it, Payne?"

Jacob grinned. "I can handle it."

"You can. Thank the Lord for that. But if you could see to it that you don't attract any more trouble in the next few weeks, I sure would appreciate it. The U.S. Marshal has left for St. Louis for some meeting or some such, so it's just us for a bit."

"Santos is gone?"

"Yeah. It's nothing we can't handle, of course. I'm just asking you not to bring in anything extra."

"I'll do my best, Deputy," Jacob said.

"We're counting on you. Gotta keep those outlaws in line." The deputy chuckled. "Well, friend, I'll leave you to your night. None of these boys will have any fun if they know a deputy is hanging around."

Jacob watched Lowry cross the room and head out the door into the dusky evening. He took a deep breath and looked around. With the adrenaline rush of breaking up a fight, Jacob felt like he needed to run for miles. He assessed the room and the people he had pushed past when he first entered. His friend Edwin was playing cards over by the front window. He recognized another circle of men drinking and laughing in the corner nearby.

Jacob had come to the Golden Saddle Saloon to relax for the evening, and that hadn't happened yet.

He needed a beer.

Before he could take more than two steps toward the bar, however, he was interrupted by a scream piercing the night.

"Help! Please, help!" a familiar voice cried.

Jacob darted through the crowd toward the sound, adrenaline pumping once more.

CHAPTER TWO

"Help!" Holly cried. "Oh, please, someone! Help!"

She had rushed down the stairs from the floor above and now leaned far over the railing, calling for anyone to come to her aid. The men closest to the stairs looked at her in stunned bewilderment. That might have been the whiskey dulling their reactions. Jacob rushed to her and clasped her outstretched hand.

"What is it? What's happened?"

"I found . . . I found . . ." She burst into tears and shook her head, unable to say another word.

"Show me," Jacob said gently.

Holly nodded and wrapped her fingers around his bicep as he led her back upstairs.

Jacob leaned into the hysterical woman and tried to soothe her. Clearly whatever she had found or witnessed was traumatic for her, and he wanted to help calm her just for her own sake. But, also, if he needed more information, he certainly wouldn't get it out of her in this state.

When they reached the top of the stairs, Jacob noticed that one of the doors halfway down the hallway was standing ajar. Though he had not been a client of Holly's girls the whole time he had been in Tucson, he knew enough to find that invasion of privacy out of the ordinary.

Holly clutched Jacob's arm harder, digging her fingernails into his muscle, and froze in place at the top of the stairs. The bounty hunter looked from her face to the open door and back again; her fear was unmistakable.

"Are we going to that room?" he asked.

She swallowed and nodded, still not averting her eyes from the target. He began to take a step down the hallway, but she held him in place.

"Holly," he said gently. "Do you want to stay here?"

She finally dragged her eyes away from the open door to look at him. With a shaky smile and another nod, she finally let go of his arm.

"Okay," Jacob said. "I'll go check it out. I need you to do something for me, though."

Holly nodded, some of her usual resolve finding its way back into her eyes.

"I need you to make sure no one else goes in there. Check on your girls in these other rooms. Don't let anyone come up the stairs. I need your help on this, okay?"

"Yes. I can do that." Her voice was barely above a whisper, yet she didn't hesitate.

"Thank you." Jacob put his big hand on her shoulder and gave her a reassuring squeeze. He hoped that giving her a responsibility like this would help distract her from whatever horror he was about to walk into.

The open doorway was still far enough down the hall that from this angle he had no idea what was inside. The door was ajar about a foot. As Jacob took the final step and stood in the doorframe, he inhaled deeply, steeling himself.

He reached out and slowly pushed the door all the way open.

As it swung in the half circle, the door snagged on something lying on the floor. Another gentle push from Jacob and it pulled clear of the obstacle and opened completely.

Jacob's breath caught in his throat.

Sprawled across the floor lay the man Randall had called Timson, on his stomach, with a growing pool of blood spreading toward the bed.

Jacob rushed forward, using both hands to turn the man over. He was still warm. Whatever had occurred, Holly had only just missed being part of it. Jacob passed his hands over the man's injuries, identifying what appeared to be several different stab wounds. Jacob's bloodied fingers felt Timson's neck for a pulse.

"He's dead," a deep, gravelly voice said.

Jacob whirled around, acutely aware that his hands were covered in blood. In the doorway stood Randall Hall.

"Call a doctor!"

"There's no point, Payne."

"How do you know?"

"I checked. Don't forget this is my establishment. I heard Holly scream before she ran downstairs and came to see what was upsetting her."

Jacob raked his eyes over the saloon-owner's appearance. He spotted a small, dark spot on the man's right cuff, but he otherwise seemed untouched. "How did you manage to check he was dead and get so little blood on you?"

Randall shrugged. "I just stayed away from the wounds. I checked for a pulse first."

"You didn't try to see if you could save him?"

"With that amount of blood lost?"

Jacob nodded grimly. There was a pragmatic logic to that, even if it went against what he himself had done instinctually.

"Well, did you see anything else?" he asked. "If you were here right after Holly, surely you saw someone leave the room."

"Only Holly," he said pointedly.

"All right," Jacob said. He didn't want to pursue that line of investigation just yet. "What can you tell me about this man?"

"Bob Timson? What have you heard?"

"Nothing," Jacob said, ignoring the suspicion he heard in the other man's voice. "I only just met him tonight. Downstairs. When he was getting into that fight. He didn't make a great impression on me, to be honest."

"Yeah, he seems to have a bit of a temper." Randall leaned against the doorframe and crossed his arms in front of his chest. "Or seemed, rather."

"You've seen him in other fights?"

Randall shrugged. "Sure. But I've seen most of the men downstairs in at least one fight. Timson's no different."

"Any idea who might have done this then?"

"Nope." Randall dug a fingernail between his two front teeth. "Not that I can tell. The man's only been in town a week."

"Right. And, I'm sorry, I never did catch why he was in town. He wasn't planning to stay?"

"Nope," Randall said again. "He's a salesman. I think those trunks in the corner are full of his wares, brought out here from the east. I heard him say there's more money to be made selling pickaxes to miners than there is in the gold they're mining."

Jacob nodded. He knew men just like that: men who would take advantage of another's desperation or naivety; men like Jacob's own brother.

Nevertheless, men like that didn't deserve to be killed.

Jacob looked around the room, hoping some clue, some detail, would jump out at him. His eyes fell on the washstand in the corner. In the internal battle over disturbing the scene of the crime and contaminating everything with blood, Jacob's responsible self won out. He stepped gingerly around the corpse and toward the washstand.

But in the few feet between body and washstand, another clue caught his eye. It was a small, dark spot soaking into the wooden floor board—likely blood. The quilt from the twin bed was hanging off, onto the floor, covering most of the blood stain. Mindful of the blood already on his hands, Jacob nudged aside the quilt with the toe of his boot.

There, mostly hidden under the victim's bed, was a long, narrow knife. The entire blade and halfway up the pearl handle, even to the small decorative stones, was covered in blood. Bob Timson's blood, no doubt.

From behind him, Randall let out a low whistle. "Would you look at that?"

Jacob let the quilt fall back where it was and continued his task of washing the blood off his hands. This situation was only becoming more complicated; he needed to begin his investigation.

As he dried his wet hands on the front of his shirt, he looked around the room again. He didn't want to disturb anything in case the deputies needed it for an investigation, but at the same time, there wasn't a moment to lose.

"Did you send someone to the sheriff's office?" he asked Randall.

"Oh. Not yet. You're right. I'll go do that."

Randall left Jacob alone in the room to go

over the dead man's personal effects. Starting back at the door to the room and slowly turning clockwise, Jacob gave the entire space a once-over.

This room was larger than most hotel rooms he had been in. This was likely due to it being used for more long-term stays, or even for one of Holly's girls to live in. Jacob didn't know the details of the business—or personal—relationship between Randall and Holly, but however they had arranged things was working out for them so far. It had allowed this room to be available for Bob Timson to live in while he stayed in Tucson.

Jacob didn't know exactly what he was looking for, but he had to start somewhere.

The washstand held a single, shallow drawer. Inside Jacob found three bobby pins, a comb, a clean handkerchief, and a dime. Nothing that pointed to a motive or any reason the man on the floor would have been attacked at all, let alone killed. There was a short stack of papers on the bedside table, mostly receipts for travel from the last several months. Jacob scanned quickly, but nothing in the information stood out to him. Nothing that seemed significant.

Other than stripping the sheets from the bed, the last place Jacob saw to search was the pile of trunks in the corner. Without opening every single one of them, it was impossible to tell which was the man's personal items, and which was his inventory. But that didn't matter. Jacob was a thorough investigator. He opened the topmost trunk and got to work.

It was a slow process. Many of the objects were wrapped in other objects, nested inside each other, stacked gently. Primarily household wares, luxuries that women might miss from keeping house back east and be able to talk their husbands into replacing for whatever exorbitant cost Timson could charge. Impractically fancy tea sets and handheld mirrors with gold filigree handles. A bundle of letters that Jacob skimmed through but which yielded nothing useful.

He pulled out the last item, a roll of green ribbon, from the final trunk and turned it over in his hand. Not a single thing in this collection had given him any insight as to why Bob Timson would have been killed. No threatening note, no stolen precious object. Nothing.

"Well?" Randall asked as he entered. "I've got a boy running to find a deputy now. Find anything?"

"Hmm . . ." Jacob searched again, this time more slowly and methodically. He set aside each item he came across into a neat pile on the bed, making sure he went through every drawer, bag, and chest thoroughly. But again, nothing.

"Are you looking for something specific?"

Jacob didn't respond. He had reached the end of his search of the room. The only thing left to search was the corpse. Though he had had plenty of dealings with dead bodies, both in the war and after, he still never liked to disturb a man's final rest.

The bounty hunter said a silent prayer asking forgiveness for what he was about to do, then checked the dead man's pockets. His coat was easy to search, especially once Jacob had moved the body onto its back. But when Jacob had to check the man's pants pockets, he grimaced at having to turn the body over again.

And still nothing but a small cigarette case he left alone.

Though he had only met the man less than an hour earlier, Jacob knew what he should be looking for.

"So?" Randall shifted his weight. "What do you think?"

Jacob returned to his feet. He had again bloodied his hands in his search of the man's clothing, but that was the least of his concerns now. He wiped his fingers on the legs of his pants as he turned back to Randall.

"You say Timson has been here a week. In that time, did you happen to notice his billfold? Maybe when he paid for a drink or tipped one of the girls?"

Randall nodded, glancing around the room Jacob had just searched. "I did. The one with the rose on it, right? And full of more greenbacks than I have ever seen in one place in my life."

"Right. Well. It's missing. Greenbacks and all."

CHAPTER THREE

"What's missing?" Deputy Lowry stood in the doorway, just behind Randall. His face wore an expression of pure fury; he seemed not to notice that he was physically pushing the saloon proprietor out of his way.

"This man had a billfold full of cash not thirty minutes ago," Jacob explained, "and I can't seem to locate it at all now."

"Well, I guess we'll have to look again."

"I searched the whole room, Deputy. Twice, in fact. It's not here."

"We'll see." Lowry strode into the room, stepping over the corpse without a glance and moving to the unpacked trunks in the corner.

"Wait, Deputy." Jacob put both hands on the man's chest, which served to stop him in his tracks and force him to listen to the bounty hunter. "We're talking about a murdered man here. He deserves our respect."

"I have an investigation to conduct."

"But won't it be easier to search the room once he has been moved? Let's call the coroner, and while the body is being taken care of I can fill you in on what I found."

"Hm. Maybe . . ."

"Here. Look." Jacob lifted up the edge of the quilt to show where the knife had heretofore been hidden. "That's probably the weapon. Let's start with that."

Deputy Lowry begrudgingly acquiesced, as he kneeled to look more carefully. "You might be right, Payne." Delicately lifting the weapon by the bit that had not been bloodied, the deputy examined it, before wrapping it in a discarded towel and tucking it into his jacket. "Let's start with what we already know. Come on."

He led them over the body and out the door. As they headed down the hallway, Jacob stopped Randall for one last question.

"Where's Holly?"

Randall shook his head darkly. "I had one of her girls put her to bed. She's had quite the shock and won't be good for anything until she has a good rest."

"We'll want to question her. Send word as soon as she recovers, will you?"

Randall nodded. "Sure will. I have some questions of my own for her."

"And keep anyone out of this room except the coroner," Lowry said. "I'll send him to you as soon as I can."

"Of course, Deputy," Randall said. "I'll take care of it."

Down the stairs they went, past the curious glances of the drinking regulars crowding the saloon on a Saturday night. The bounty hunter and the deputy both studiously ignored the interest and calls for information that were hurled at them. Out the door to the boardwalk lining the main street, and the pair turned in silent agreement to walk up the road toward a more private location.

"Are we going to the sheriff's office?" Jacob asked.

Lowry shook his head. "We've got two men locked up in the jail right now. I don't need them overhearing. Let's go to the cafe. I bet Bonnie will find us a quiet corner."

In just a few short moments they had

walked to the San Xavier Cafe, which was also crowded, this being Saturday night after all. But after a whispered conversation with the bartender, Bonnie led the two into the cramped, hot kitchen behind the bar. Jacob stood in the doorway and looked around while the deputy scooted behind the one narrow table.

"Is everything all right?" Bonnie stood behind Jacob, peeking over his shoulder anxiously. "Jacob . . ." She lowered her voice. "Where did that blood come from?"

He heard the unmistakable panic in her voice, but hesitated to answer immediately. Jacob exchanged a glance with Deputy Lowry. How much of this needed to remain a secret? How much would be revealed as they interviewed witnesses or suspects? The deputy nodded, giving him the go-ahead.

"Don't worry," Jacob said to the hovering waitress. "It's not my blood. I'm fine."

She nodded and let out a slow breath.

"But," Jacob continued, "there's been a death."

"No!"

"I'm not sure . . . you might have met him. Mr. Bob Timson? The traveling salesman been in Tucson for the last week?"

"Mr. Timson?" Bonnie dropped the empty

tin mug she had been holding. The clatter as it hit the wooden floorboards shook her out of her shock. "Why, yes! He came in here almost every day. He was awfully kind to me, even though I got the sense he didn't like many other people. He's dead?" Her gaze drifted down over the bloodstains on Jacob's pants again. "What happened?"

"Well, that's what we're trying to figure out," Deputy Lowry said. "You say you know Timson? Why don't you sit down and tell us what you know about him?"

"I—" Bonnie glanced over her shoulder to the dining room of the cafe. Mickey, the bartender, caught her eye and gestured for her to go ahead.

Jacob stepped to the side of the doorway and put a gentle hand on her elbow to guide her to the table. "Just anything you can remember, Bonnie. Even if you don't think it's important."

She nodded and swallowed as she lowered herself into the only other chair.

"You're sure you're okay?" she asked Jacob.

Jacob smiled reassuringly. "I'm sure. Go ahead, Bonnie. Is there anything you can tell us about that man's time in town? Did he make any enemies that you know of? You said he didn't seem to like other people? Did you pick up anything out of the ordinary in your conversations with him?"

"Every time he came in he was so kind to me. Mickey always told me Mr. Timson was flirting with me, but I didn't see it."

With that deflection, Bonnie blushed, and Jacob noticed she wouldn't meet his eyes. He certainly couldn't blame the other man for giving this woman special attention when he ate here.

"He seemed to have very little patience for anyone else," she went on. "I could always tell when he had lost money at the poker table because he seemed to lash out at everyone. Lucky in particular."

"What do you mean by 'lash out'?" Lowry asked.

She darted her eyes between the two men, as though worried she had said something wrong. "Well, just . . . I mean . . ."

"Did he yell at Lucky?" Jacob prompted. "Threaten him at all?"

Bonnie nodded. "He did. Both of those things. In fact, the last time they were both in here at the same time, they got into a shoving match by the door. I wasn't close enough to hear what was said. I only know that I turned my back for one moment and then I heard someone crashing into a table and falling to the floor. Somehow Timson, who must be almost a foot shorter, had managed to knock Lucky over, he was that mad."

"But you don't know what they were arguing about?"

"Not that time. But before . . ." She looked away from the men, her eyes searching her memory. "I think the day or two before that was when Mr. Timson accused Lucky of stealing from him. And another day earlier that week was when he shouted at both Abe and Lucky about cheating. That one actually happened in the street in front of the cafe, though."

"Outside? Do you think other people witnessed it?"

"Oh, yes. There was already a crowd gathered by the time Mickey and I got out there."

"How did that one end?"

"Mr. Hall happened to be walking by and he and Mickey managed to calm them down."

"Hall? Randall was there?"

She nodded. "He seemed to know Mr. Timson pretty well. At least well enough to know what to say to him to soothe his temper."

"And what did Lucky and Abe do?"

A cloud flitted across her expression and her

eyes widened. "They kept shouting. Or, Abe did. Lucky just looked . . ." She trailed off.

Jacob and Deputy Lowry exchanged a glance. "It's all right, Miss Loft," the deputy said. "You can tell us. You're safe."

"Lucky looked fearsome," she said almost in a whisper. "I have never seen such a look on his face. I don't know what he would have done if Mr. Hall hadn't come and walked Mr. Timson back to the saloon."

After a pause, Jacob pressed further. "Is there anything else you can tell us, Bonnie? Can you think of anyone else who might have been angry at Mr. Timson?"

She shook her head, furrowing her brow as she thought. "No one that I can remember at the moment." She turned to Lowry. "I'm sorry, Deputy. I try not to get involved in all the men's conflicts."

"Of course, Miss Loft." He took her hand in his across the table. "I completely understand—"

"Oh, but," she cut in, "there was one other. Just a couple days ago a stranger bumped into Mr. Timson near the doorway. I didn't hear what they said to each other, but there was definitely anger and some accusations thrown."

"What did this stranger look like?" Jacob asked.

"Let me think . . . tall and skinny with dirty, dark hair."

"That sounds familiar," Jacob said to the deputy. "I think I know who that was."

"Good." Lowry nodded. "Sounds like we have plenty of people to follow up with. Miss Loft, you've been most helpful. If there's anything else you remember about Mr. Timson's time here in Tucson, you'll let me know?"

She nodded, and sat up straighter. "I will. Of course, Deputy. Do you think it's all right if I get back to my tables? I hate to let the other girl handle all of it."

"Go ahead. Thank you again. We may be in touch."

Bonnie smiled shyly at Jacob and Lowry as she rose from the table. She grabbed her empty serving tray and exited the kitchen, intent on her job.

While Jacob watched her leave, Deputy Lowry let out a long, slow breath. "It sounds like we're dealing with a man who didn't care much what other people thought of him. Which makes for a conspicuous target, I guess."

Jacob shook his head in disbelief. "It never fails to amaze me how men from back east will come out here and not realize how far they are from the law they are used to."

Lowry snorted. "Those are the type of men who think their money will fix anything."

"In Boston, I'm sure Timson was used to a streetlight on every corner, men who respected the law and his position. Here, though?"

"Well," the deputy said with a sigh, "he learned a hard lesson.

"But he didn't deserve what he got," Jacob said.

Lowry nodded. "Tell me about what you found in that room."

In a few sentences, Jacob summarized for the deputy what he had found, what he had not found, the condition of the body when it was discovered, both Holly's and Randall's behavior, and the two men he had witnessed watching the fight—one with dark, dirty hair, one with peculiar green boots.

"Well. That seems like plenty to get started with. Appreciate your help, Payne. You mind coming to speak to the coroner with me?"

"Happy to. Anything I can do to help."

As the two men exited the tiny kitchen, past the bar again, Mickey called to them.

"Ay. You boys talking about Timson, are ya? I can tell you some things."

CHAPTER FOUR

Jacob leaned far over the bar at San Xavier Cafe, getting as close to the bartender as he could, and whispered, "You know something about Bob Timson? Bonnie just told us about the fights he has gotten into here."

Mickey nodded. "More than just fights, lads. More than words. I saw him waving a weapon about."

"You best not be lying, Mick," Deputy Lowry warned. "This is a murder investigation and I can't have anyone obstructing justice."

"And what good would it be for me to lie now, eh?" Mickey glanced over his shoulder at the new arrivals at the other end of the bar. "Pull up a stool here, boys. I'll be right back."

Once the older man was out of earshot,

Jacob said quietly, "I've not known Mickey to make up stories. But what kind of man would wave a weapon around a quiet cafe like this one?"

"The kind of man gonna get himself murdered," Deputy Lowry answered. "I'm interested to hear what Mickey has to say, at least."

Two shot glasses of whiskey appeared on the bar, the one in front of Jacob sloshing over the lip and spilling down the side of the glass. He looked up to see Mickey had joined them again.

"Can't leave my post, boys. You understand. So you sit here and drink like any other customer and we'll talk."

Lowry tossed back his whiskey as Jacob leaned forward to whisper again. "Tell us what you saw, Mickey. Was Timson really going around threatening people with a gun?"

"He was, just that, lads." Mickey glanced down the bar at the next closest drinker before continuing. " 'Twas a knife, though. Not a gun."

"What?" Deputy Lowry cleared his throat. "Did you say a *knife*?"

Jacob tossed back his own shot of whiskey. This whole situation was getting somber.

Mickey nodded. "I didn't get a real good look at it, but it didn't seem to be like any knife I've ever seen. Not out here, at least. Seemed like the kind of namby-pamby fancy knife a man might buy in Boston just for show."

Lowry grinned. "Yeah, I can imagine. Do you think you'd recognize it again if you saw it?"

"Aye. 'Twas unique enough. Long and narrow. Looked more like a letter opener than a knife, I'm thinking. But the handle had a few decorative stones in it. Like I said, fancy."

Jacob and Lowry exchanged a look, but neither gave anything more away to the bartender. The fewer people who knew the details of the murder the better, but the fact that the man seemed to have been killed by his own weapon opened up another big line of questioning.

"When was this?" Jacob asked. "And who was he threatening?"

"Just a couple days ago, I'm thinking. No more than three. I didn't recognize the man he was speaking to, but he's been around since then. Blond fella, mustache. Otherwise unre-markable."

Jacob stopped him. "Did he happen to be wearing green boots?"

Mickey nodded as he stepped away to answer an order from another patron.

"You know who he means, Payne?"

"Yeah. Could be. Those fellas I told you

about, the strangers watching Timson. One matches this description. The other matches the one Bonnie gave us of that stranger Timson fought. Sounds like he was making enemies in every direction."

"Could he have been targeted? This team or pair or whoever they are, following him from whatever town he was in last?"

"Maybe. I only saw them for a moment, but I'm not sure they were together. It might just be a coincidence. It might just be that Timson makes himself a target wherever he goes. Seems everyone has a story about him getting into disagreements, don't they?"

Lowry nodded. "I think we'll need to talk to Hall next. We should find out how Timson spent his time and when he was coming and going."

"Mickey!" Jacob called down to get the bartender's attention. "We've gotta go, but keep an eye out for us, will you?"

"Sure will." He nodded at the bounty hunter over the shoulder of the man he was serving. "I'll send word if I hear anything."

Jacob dropped a handful of coins on the bar for him before following Lowry out the door.

As the pair stepped out into the street in front of the cafe, Deputy Lowry lit a cigarette and took a long drag. Jacob had seen this before. The deputy tended to smoke more when he was unsure or anxious. While helping to investigate this murder technically wasn't Jacob's job, at the sight of the cigarette the bounty hunter knew that the other man would likely welcome his help.

"Coroner next?" he asked. "Surely he has had time for a cursory look by now."

Deputy Lowry nodded. "At least enough to confirm what we think."

Jacob led the way down the darkening street. The coroner's office on the far corner of the intersection was one of the very few buildings still with an interior light on at this time of night. A few short minutes later they were admitted into the office's back room, where the corpse of Bob Timson lay on the examination table. His clothes had been stripped off and lay in a chaotic pile on a side table, and the blood from his wounds had been cleaned from the skin.

Jacob took in the whole of the scene and details at a glance as Lowry introduced him to the county coroner, a slight, pale man in glasses.

"I'm surprised you haven't met before," the deputy said. "Jacob Payne is one of this area's most valuable bounty hunters."

"Martin Sylvester," the man said, shaking Jacob's hand. "Shame we're meeting under these circumstances."

"I agree, Mr. Sylvester. It's helpful you were able to take this on a Saturday night."

He shrugged. "It needs to be done. Might as well be now rather than later."

"Find anything we can use?" the deputy asked.

Sylvester nodded, moving around to the far side of the body. "As you can see, we have five separate wounds in the man's torso. One of them"—he pointed with a scalpel—"is actually a double entry wound. The attacker somehow managed to stab twice in the same place."

"So," Lowry clarified, "six separate stabs."

"Yep." Sylvester moved to the head of the body. "Two of the wounds must have reached his lungs. We're looking for a knife at least six inches long. You can see here"—he pointed again—"that the man lived long enough for the blood in his lungs to be coughed up."

The detective and Jacob exchanged a glance. Seems the wounds sure might fit the knife they had already found.

Jacob noticed the dried blood at the corners of Timson's mouth and shut his eyes. No matter what this man had done, no one deserved to die coughing up their own blood.

Sylvester continued as Jacob opened his eyes again.

"Now, you see this bruise on his bicep?"

"Wait." Jacob held up one hand, pausing the conversation. "Before we get too much further into the inquiry, let's clear up one thing. Mr. Sylvester, is it at all possible that this man took his own life?"

"Really, Payne?" Lowry asked with a scoffing laugh. "You think he did this himself?"

"Let him answer," Jacob said.

The coroner furrowed his brow and spit a glob of tobacco into his mug without taking his eyes off Jacob. "What are you insinuating? You doubt my analysis?"

"No. No, not at all. I'm interested in your professional opinion about the method of death."

Sylvester cleared his throat. "It is my professional opinion that this man died at the hand of someone who stabbed him six times, likely after grabbing him by the arm hard enough to bruise."

"Why are you even asking?" Lowry sputtered.

"Something doesn't feel right about this," Jacob answered cautiously. "Something about the way the body was found makes me think we are being led in the wrong direction. As though some part of it were staged or . . . I don't know. I just wanted to rule out the possibility absolutely."

"I find it hard to believe that any man would be capable of stabbing himself six times. Maybe two or three, but six seems beyond someone's physical capability." Sylvester leaned back against the table where Timson's clothes were as he continued. "But even beyond that, the angle of these wounds precludes any possibility of them being self-inflicted. No, sir. Someone else wanted this man dead."

Jacob nodded. "Thank you. That's what I wanted to clarify."

Deputy Lowry pressed on. "Did you find anything else on the body?"

Sylvester nodded to the pile of torn and bloody clothes beside him. "There was nothing in his pockets but a fancy cigarette case, and even that was empty. It's possible his killer emptied his pockets."

"It's also possible he emptied his own," Jacob suggested. "We found him in his own sleeping quarters, so maybe he was turning in for the night."

"Either way," Lowry said, "we're still missing his billfold. If Sylvester didn't find it on his person anywhere, that needs to be added to the list of questions to be answered."

Jacob grimaced. "That list just seems to be getting longer."

Lowry turned back to the coroner. "Do you still have more to do, Sylvester?"

The coroner nodded. "I can pull some more details for you. I'll let you know if I find anything worthwhile."

"Appreciate it," Lowry said.

"I guess it's time we head back to the saloon," Jacob suggested. "Maybe if we can trace Timson's final moments the solution will get clearer."

Lowry nodded. "I reckon you're right."

CHAPTER FIVE

Jacob and Deputy Lowry could hear the Golden Saddle Saloon's rowdy patrons all the way from the street outside. A mere murder upstairs hadn't dampened anyone's spirits; the men still had their quota of whiskey to drink on this Saturday night. They had continued their raucous gathering unperturbed.

Upon entering, it only took a quick glance around the room for Jacob to see that Holly had not returned. Jacob wondered if she was still in bed from the shock; he hoped she would recover soon. Her girls were still playing hostess to the drunk men and doing their job well. Even as they stood near the doorway, Jacob watched a giggling blonde latch on to her man's arm, her bosom pressed close against him. The lecherous man grinned into her face. Jacob could imagine the smell of alcohol coming off him as he let her lead him up the stairs.

"I don't see Randall down here," Lowry said. He had been scanning the room himself, while Jacob watched the salacious transaction. "We should head up to the room."

Jacob nodded. "Hope we can get some information out of Randall before he's too far gone."

Lowry threw him a grim look then led the way across the crowded room. He politely but firmly turned aside two girls who moved to greet them.

"Not tonight, ladies." He winked at them as they passed.

Jacob only nodded and followed close behind the deputy to the foot of the stairs. Once they had climbed to the second floor, the noise diminished some, though muffled laughter, the tinkle of piano keys, and glasses being knocked into each other floated up the stairwell. They made their way down the hallway to where Timson's door still sat wide open.

"Doesn't seem like he did anything to secure the room, did he?" Jacob said.

"Can I help you? You find anything of interest?"

Jacob turned to find Randall Hall just behind him, looking over his shoulder into the empty room.

"Has anyone been in here?" Deputy Lowry asked, using his thumb to point over his shoulder.

"Not so far as I know."

"But you left the door open?" Jacob clarified.

Randall shrugged. "I mean . . . you told me not to disturb anything, so I didn't. I didn't know you wanted the door closed."

Jacob resisted sighing at such logic, but only barely. "Has anyone been put on watch? Do you know for sure no one has been in here?"

"Well, I . . . uh . . ." Randall looked farther down the hallway as though checking for other people before continuing. "I did leave to go check on things downstairs, but I don't think anyone has been in here."

"Mr. Hall." Jacob recognized Lowry had just put on his most intimidating voice as the deputy loomed over the other man. "I told you specifically to keep this room secure and you failed to do so. If you have in any way compromised this investigation, I will hold you personally responsible. I can assure you that won't be good for your business."

"Yes, sir," Randall said meekly. "You're right, sir."

"So." Jacob finally released his sigh. "It's possible someone was in here, huh?" He stood in the doorway and took a careful look around the room. From this standpoint it didn't appear as though anything had been disturbed, although he couldn't be certain. "Everything seems fine at first glance," he told the deputy.

"All right, then. Hall, we've got some questions for you."

"Of course. Yes, of course." The man nodded vigorously. "Why don't we go down to my office?"

"And leave the room unguarded again?" Jacob asked.

Randall blinked. "Oh."

Lowry rolled his eyes. "Here is fine, Hall. Any guests of yours who come upstairs will just have to deal with the sight of a sheriff's deputy in your establishment."

"Yes, sir."

"Let's start with how long the victim has been a resident here."

"Well, I . . ." Randall rubbed his chin thoughtfully. "I'd have to check my records, but I'd guess near a week. Maybe nine days."

"And what were his habits while staying here?"

"He was a bit of an early riser. I'd run into him as early as seven in the morning some days, and then not see him again until mid-afternoon."

"Know where he was spending his days?" Jacob asked.

Randall shook his head. "Some days he'd leave with one of his traveling cases, but I don't know if he was just going door to door, or if he had appointments places. Some days he didn't even take any of his wares."

Jacob turned to the deputy. "Is it possible the salesman act was a front for something more?"

Lowry shrugged. "Could be. Some of that stuff you found doesn't really seem like the kind of product a good businessman would haul about the country."

Jacob nodded. "I wonder how much of this all was his, and how much was for sale. Maybe he was looking for a place to settle down."

"Yeah," Randall said eagerly. "That sounds right. I seem to remember him mentioning a woman left back in Boston."

"Really?" Jacob was skeptical, but he couldn't put his finger on why.

"That might explain some of the letters you found," Lowry suggested.

Jacob didn't want to say anything more in front of the saloon proprietor. He was itching to get back in that room and do another thorough search with this new insight.

"What else can you tell us about Mr. Timson?" he asked.

Randall paused, then said, "Well, I'm not sure. Sure can't think of why anyone would want to stab him, though."

Jacob and the deputy exchanged another glance. "How did you know he had been stabbed?"

"I found the body, didn't I? Did you find the knife?"

Lowry nodded before Jacob could stop him. He pulled the handkerchief-wrapped weapon out of his inner pocket and showed it to the other man.

Randall blanched. "Oh no. It was *that* knife? That, uh . . ."

"You've seen this knife before?" Jacob asked.

The man nodded solemnly. "But I'm not sure I should say. I don't want to get anyone in trouble."

Deputy Lowry placed his hand on the proprietor's shoulder. "I understand your hesitation, Randall. I do. But we need to know every-thing about Bob Timson we can find if we have any hope of solving his murder and catching his killer before they strike again."

The man rubbed the back of his neck and frowned. "Well. As I say, I don't want to be getting anyone in trouble. But I have seen the knife, and Timson wasn't the one holding it."

"You say you saw someone else using this knife?" Lowry clarified. "Would you swear to it?"

Randall nodded. "It probably was nothing. I may be mistaken."

"What did you see?" Jacob asked.

"Well . . ." Randall shot a look down the hallway again before continuing. "The man seemed a bit sweet on Holly. Especially in the last few days. Kept trying to get her to have dinner with him or making up some reason he wanted her to come into his room. She told me about it and laughed it off, but I got the idea she didn't relish the attention."

He shot another furtive glance around before continuing.

"Just a couple days ago, I was walking down this very hallway and I heard a conversation going on in there." He pointed to the dead man's bedroom without looking. "I heard

Holly's voice, but I didn't linger. She was laughing and seemed pleased, but when I passed the doorway I saw what they were doing. Holly said something about 'loving it' or 'loving that,' and then I saw her reach for that knife."

"You saw Holly Merritt handling this knife just a couple days ago?" Jacob said incredulously.

"Yep. I think maybe Timson was showing it to her, or trying to impress her in some way. She seemed to really like it." Randall shrugged. "Otherwise, I haven't seen that knife."

"Hmm . . ." Deputy Lowry pursed his lips and glanced at Jacob. The bounty hunter couldn't read the other man's expression, but he had a feeling they'd be having further conversations about this little piece of information.

"Thanks, Randall," Jacob said. "That's very helpful."

Deputy Lowry redirected the conversation. "Any altercations you can think of? Defining characteristics? Reasons someone might come after him?"

Randall looked thoughtful before shaking his head. "No, sir. Like I told you, he was gone most of the days. I didn't notice him doing much at night. Sometimes he went over to the cafe, sometimes he gambled—a lot, actually—or maybe he had a lady friend or something."

"Didn't you just tell us you thought he had a woman back in Boston?" Jacob asked.

"Oh, well . . ." Randall shrugged. "Like I said. I don't know what he was doing. I don't think I have anything else useful for you. And"—he looked longingly down the hall toward the stairs—"if it's all the same to you gentlemen, I need to get back to work. Saturday night is a busy time here."

"Yes. Fine. Go," Lowry said with a wave of his hand. "I might have more questions for you, though."

"You know where to find me, Deputy."

Deputy Lowry and Jacob stood quietly listening as the man's footsteps faded down the stairs.

Jacob took a step into the bedroom and gave the scene another close look. With the trunks all unpacked in the corner, it was difficult to tell if anything was missing or disturbed. He realized he should have taken a better inventory, should have tried to fix it all more carefully in his memory.

"What do you think?" Lowry asked him, stepping into the room after him.

"Hard to say. I'm not sure what to make of

the fact that both Bonnie and Mickey witnessed Timson get into fights, but that Randall claims not to."

"Yeah." Lowry lifted the edge of the bedspread and folded it back over the bed. The small blood stain where the knife had been lying stood out against the wooden floor.

"Think we should check in on Holly?" Jacob asked.

Lowry nodded, but frowned. "We do need to talk to her. But she might also need to recover from the shock. Maybe it can wait till tomorrow. I don't know how much use she'll be if she's actually sick."

Jacob nodded. "Might be a chance she's avoiding us. Claiming to be ill to get out of being questioned."

"You think she'd do that?"

He shrugged. "Could be. She's smart. If she had anything to do with this, she'd have thought of a way out of it."

"I suppose you're right about that."

Jacob glanced back through the doorway at the sound of footsteps. Both he and Lowry fell quiet, listening and watching. After a few short moments, one of the strangers Jacob had noticed downstairs earlier stood in the doorway.

His dirty dark hair hung over his face, but Jacob still saw his expression of surprise.

"Oh, shi—" the man said, and spun around to leave.

"Stop!" Lowry shouted.

CHAPTER SIX

The stranger didn't stop when ordered to by Deputy Lowry, but instead kept moving back toward the end of the hall and the stairway he had just climbed. Jacob didn't hesitate; he shoved the deputy to one side and darted after the man. The thud behind him told Jacob that Lowry had slammed into the wall, but he didn't have time to apologize. The stranger was getting away.

The hallway was short, too short for Jacob to be able to give much chase, but when the skinny stranger slowed at the top of the stairs, he saw his chance. Jacob took one last flying leap to tackle the other man, pushing him into the wall and pinning the target under his considerable bulk.

"Hold it," he said with a growl. "You're not going anywhere."

The stringy-haired man squirmed under Jacob's weight, trying to kick him and gain leverage against the wall at the same time. The bounty hunter was now well accustomed to the tactics of men trying to escape him and shifted his weight accordingly. He pushed his meaty forearm against the man's Adam's apple, holding him firm against the wall and waited for the stranger to give up the struggle.

"You gonna suffocate yourself?" Jacob taunted. "We just want to ask you a few questions."

When the man continued to twist and thresh, Jacob sighed and punched him in the ribs. An anguished gasp escaped him as his legs buckled.

"I didn't want to have to do that." Jacob stepped away from the man, keeping a firm grip on his arm but leaving him space to catch his breath. "I did warn you. Come on."

Without waiting for the stranger to fully recover, Jacob dragged him back up the couple steps to the second landing, where the deputy was watching with admiration.

"Nice job, Payne."

"This is the guy." Jacob shook the man's arm.

"One of the ones I noticed downstairs watching Timson earlier."

"Is he?" Lowry looked the dirty stranger up and down.

"Looks like the man Bonnie described too, huh?"

"I don't know what you're talking about," the man said, snarling. "I don't know nothin' about no Timson."

"Yeah. Sure. Let's take him down to Randall's office," Lowry said. "I bet he has plenty to tell us."

The stranger was beginning to recover his breath, as well as his strength. Jacob twisted the man's arm behind his back, holding him more securely for the march downstairs. Lowry crossed back to the dead man's room, took one more look inside, then closed the door securely behind him.

"Here." Jacob used a free hand to dig a single match out of his pocket. "Stick that between the door and the frame. That way we'll know if anyone goes in there before we get back."

Lowry started a bit; the idea took him by surprise. He nodded as he accepted the match. "You're right. Smart, Payne."

After securing the door, the deputy led the

way down the stairs, Jacob and the intruder following closely. Every few steps, Lowry glanced behind him, making sure that Jacob had not lost his grip or needed help. They descended into the main room of the saloon, where the Saturday evening shenanigans were beginning to wind down.

As they reached the foot of the stairs, the man tried again to shake off Jacob's grip.

"Let me go," he hissed under his breath. "Get off. I'll go with you, just let me walk."

Jacob smirked. Whoever this stranger was, he didn't want to be associated with the law. This man appearing in the custody of the deputy would likely injure his reputation among the other men in Tucson. Especially if he was otherwise on the right side of the law.

Jacob watched the reactions of the other men in the room as they passed through the crowd. Sure enough, some avoided looking at him; some stared openly.

About halfway through the room, Jacob spied the blond stranger in the green boots he had noticed earlier that evening, but that man didn't see him. He was deep in conversation with one of the girls. With the stranger's attention thus diverted, Jacob was able to give him a long, hard look, examining him for any detail that could shed light on the mystery. Why had he been so focused on Timson earlier that evening? Who was he and where had he come from?

In his lingering glance, Jacob noticed a dark stain on the man's shirt, near his ribs and about the size of a man's hand. In this light, and through the crowd, he couldn't be sure, but it appeared to be a smear, as though the man had wiped something off his hand onto his side.

He could be wrong, but Jacob's immediate guess was that the man had blood on his clothes. Blood that maybe he picked up somewhere else, but that had certainly appeared in the time since Jacob first entered the saloon and this all began.

"Here we go," Lowry said as they reached the doorway to the owner's office.

Jacob turned his attention back to the man in his grasp. Lowry knocked briefly and let himself in without waiting for a response from within. When the door swung open, Jacob got a clear view of Randall sitting at his desk in the middle of the room. His face registered surprise and maybe even mild panic as he pushed something from the desktop into a nearby drawer. The man stood to greet his visitors.

"Deputy—you, uh . . . What can I do for you?"

"We need the private space, Randall. I'm sure you understand. We found this piece of trash"—he nodded at the man in Jacob's grip—"trying to get into Timson's room. Gotta question him."

"Oh. Yes. All right." Randall looked around the room nervously. "I think, well . . . You have enough room in here? I could open up one of the other rooms upstairs."

"We're already here. Let's get this over with," Lowry said. "I'm going to have to ask you to leave."

Randall nodded, seeming to acquiesce easily enough. "Sure. Yeah. I'll just be outside, then."

Lowry nodded and took Randall's seat behind the desk as the other man slunk out the door. Jacob dropped his captive in the single empty chair and leaned against the closed door, blocking any escape.

"So," Lowry began, "Mister . . . ?"

"Fu—"

"Now, now. I'm sure that's not your name, nor is that kind of language necessary. We have ways of finding out and you might as well tell us now instead of after you've spent a night in jail." He shrugged. "But it doesn't matter to me."

The bedraggled man glared at Lowry, turned to glare at Jacob—and perhaps assess his chances of breaking out of the room—and then slumped back into his chair. "They call me Lenny," he said sullenly, shaking his hair back off his face. "Lenny Duffin."

Jacob wondered how much of a chance it was that "Lenny" was an alias, but he didn't press it. Instead he leaned over the man and asked, "And what are you doing in Tucson, Duffin?"

When the man didn't respond, Lowry pressed, "What were you doing in Timson's room?"

"Nothing," he grumbled.

"Must have been doing something," Jacob said. "What were you doing upstairs, if not for that?"

"You were all alone, so don't give us any stories about any girls," Lowry added.

Duffin shrugged.

Jacob nudged his chair from behind, startling the man.

"What were you doing upstairs?" Jacob repeated.

Duffin glared at Lowry, who responded with a grin.

"I've got all night," the deputy said, leaning

back in his chair and putting his feet on the desk.

Lowry held the man's glare for nearly a minute. Duffin stayed silent the whole while before turning to glare at Jacob. Neither man gave an inch or any indication they would budge. This was simply a matter of waiting him out. Jacob could lean against that door forever, waiting for the man to spill what he knew.

"Fine," Duffin finally grumbled, giving in. "I was upstairs to check out that room. But I wasn't looking for anything specific."

"Then why even bother?" Jacob asked. "Why risk it?"

Duffin shrugged again. "I dunno. I heard the guy was dead and I thought there might be something worth . . . liberating."

"Liberating?" Jacob repeated, incredulously.

Lowry scoffed. "You expect us to believe that? Jacob here saw you watching the victim earlier in the evening."

"I didn't do anything," Lenny insisted. "I was just watching the fight. The little guy was making a big fuss, wasn't he? Everyone was watching."

"How'd you hear he died?" Jacob asked.

Lenny just glared at him.

"How'd you hear he died?" he asked again.

The man shrugged. "People talk."

"Goddammit, Duffin," Lowry exclaimed. "What are you hiding? Maybe I should just lock you up now for suspicion of murder."

"Wait, no." Duffin raised his hands in surrender. "I swear. That's all. I heard the saloon owner—what's his name?"

"Randall Hall."

"Him." Duffin nodded. "I overheard him tell one of the girls that one of his best paying customers had kicked the bucket. Thought I'd check it out."

"What else did he say?"

"I didn't hear it," Duffin retorted. "I was already on my way upstairs."

"Did anyone else overhear?"

"Maybe. I don't know. I don't pay attention."

"You expect us to believe that?" Jacob asked.

"That's it," Duffin said. "That's all I know. You're wasting your time with me."

Jacob thought a moment. In spite of everything, he was inclined to believe the man. While it felt like there was certainly a few things he was hiding, it seemed that the murder of Bob Timson was not one of them. Lowry caught his eye over Duffin's head. Jacob shrugged, letting the deputy make the final call.

"All right, Duffin," Lowry said. "I'm going to

keep an eye on you, but for tonight you're free to go. If we need to ask you any more questions, I expect you to be cooperative, you hear?"

Duffin was already to his feet and halfway to the door.

"Yeah, yeah," he muttered.

Jacob stepped aside and let the man exit the office. Lowry, already back on his feet, stood in the doorway watching the strange man push his way through the crowd to the door of the saloon.

The crowd in the saloon was thinning out, men going home or to their girl's room for the evening. All that remained were the last of the revelers. Jacob spotted the stranger from earlier, blond with the green boots, still leaning over the bar and nursing his beer. From this angle the blood stain wasn't visible, but Jacob was certain he had seen it earlier.

"Know who that is?" Jacob asked, pointing out the man to the deputy.

Lowry craned his neck to see around someone else. "Not right off. He looks familiar, though."

"Wonder how long he's been in town."

Lowry nodded. "Wonder why I know his face."

"Maybe check the stack of wanted posters," Jacob suggested.

"Yeah. I will. Good thinking." Lowry shook his head. "Damn, Payne. There are always so many outlaws come through this town. I don't know how we're expected to catch up."

"Yeah, well. That's what bounty hunters are for," Jacob said with a grin. "I still don't like that we haven't had a word with Holly, though."

"You're right. I'd like to know what she saw."

"First thing tomorrow," Jacob said. "Let's meet back here and see if we can't get a word with the madam."

CHAPTER SEVEN

The following morning, Jacob strode down Tucson's main street to the sound of church bells. While other citizens were saving their souls and recovering from their late night, he was eager to make progress on this investigation. With the large number of suspects, any one of whom could leave town and escape justice at any moment, the pressure was on to solve the mystery and make an arrest.

Jacob thanked God it was Sunday. None of the stagecoach drivers would want to set out on this day, so their suspects would—should—be stuck in town until at least the next morning. He and Deputy Lowry had time. Not a lot of time, but some.

Even waiting overnight to question more

witnesses had caused him no small anxiety. If this had been a bounty he was after, he would have pushed through, following leads, waking men up if necessary as he gathered the details he needed to make his capture. But here in town, both abiding within the law and working with the citizens of Tucson, he had to go at a slower pace. He prayed it wasn't too slow.

As he walked down the street, from his small rented room to the saloon where he was to meet Deputy Lowry, Jacob reviewed the information they had gathered the night before. The victim, Bob Timson, seemed to be a man with no qualms about making enemies. Whether that was because of his own confidence in his status or because he was used to changing towns and evading conflict regularly, Jacob didn't know. But the fact remained that so far they had discovered no fewer than three different people in town who had a reason to want to hurt Timson.

If the murder weapon was the knife that had belonged to the victim, that meant that any one of the suspects would have had access to it, not to mention Holly. All they had needed to do was enter Timson's room behind him and somehow take control of it.

That meant that he and Lowry would need

to figure out which of these possible suspects was so driven by their anger or greed or whatever their motive was to follow through on the impulse.

Jacob was lost in thought and didn't realize he was already on the boardwalk in front of the Golden Saddle Saloon until he heard someone call his name.

"Payne! Wait a minute."

He turned to see Deputy Lowry walking quickly down the deserted dirt street toward him, waving a piece of paper. Immediately, Jacob's stomach was in his throat. Some new piece of information had come to light. They could be one big step closer to solving this murder.

"What did you find?"

"Look at this." Lowry reached his side and thrust the paper at him. "Just look. I told you his face was familiar."

Jacob took the proffered page and found himself staring into the dark, soulless eyes of the blond stranger he had seen the night before. The man Jacob had spotted with a wide smear of blood on his shirt was the same man that was wanted for murder in Albuquerque. Earl Pelling, just under six feet and near two hundred pounds, was under suspicion for murdering a family of five outside of the city, approximately two weeks ago. According to the bulletin Jacob held, Pelling was also wanted for questioning about the disappearance of the family's six horses, including one highly prized stallion.

"Well, look at this," Jacob said softly.

"That's him, right? That's the man you saw last night?"

"Sure looks like him." Jacob read over the man's charges again, disgusted at the horror another human being could cause.

"Wanted for murder *and* you spotted blood on his clothes? We're going to need to find this Earl Pelling fella."

Jacob nodded. "Maybe Randall knows where to find him, since every visitor to Tucson ends up coming through this saloon eventually."

"Seems like we got plenty to do this morn-ing." Lowry took the wanted poster back, folded it, and stuffed it in an interior jacket pocket. He pushed the saloon door open and gestured for Jacob to follow him.

"We're closed," a thin voice called to them as they stepped through the door. "Come back at midday."

"Sheriff's Deputy Lowry," he said, flashing his badge. "We have some questions. Were you here last night?"

The heavyset, balding man approached the end of the bar nearest the door where Jacob and Lowry had entered. He eyed the proffered badge before saying, "I'll get Mr. Hall for you."

"Wait," Jacob said. "What about *you*? Did you work last night?"

"What's your name, sir?" Lowry asked.

"Buddy." He looked back to where Randall's office door stood closed. "Buddy Lanham. And I wasn't here last night."

Lowry leaned over the bar toward him. Buddy took a step back.

"Did you hear anything about what happened last night, Buddy? Anything seem different this morning?"

The man shrugged.

"Mr. Hall didn't tell you any news?" Jacob pressed, stepping up beside Lowry. "Have you seen Ms. Merritt yet this morning?"

Buddy sucked at his front teeth. "Should I get Mr. Hall for you?"

"Yeah," Lowry said. "Get him. But we're not done with you."

Jacob and the deputy made themselves comfortable on barstools while the taciturn man fetched his employer.

"If it wasn't him," Jacob said, "we could find

the bartender working last night. He probably talked to Pelling if nothing else."

"What can I help you gentlemen with?" they heard from across the room.

When Jacob looked up, Randall was quickly striding toward them. His expression looked pained; his welcoming smile seemed forced. That was understandable. He had had a murder investigation going on in his place of business for the last twelve hours. It must be trying.

"Randall," Lowry said, offering his hand to shake. "Thank you for meeting with us again. We just have a few more questions. Should we go to your office?"

The deputy moved to walk to the back of the saloon, but Randall stopped him.

"Here is fine," he said impatiently. "It's fine. What are your questions?"

"Has Ms. Merritt been down yet this morning?" Jacob began. "We still need to speak to her about what she saw last night."

"Not yet. Although . . ." Randall trailed off and glanced at the foot of the stairs. Jacob saw his body stiffen a tiny bit. Something had shifted in the man's mind, a decision reached or choice made. He lowered his voice. "I feel like I should warn you boys about her, while we have a moment."

"What do you mean?"

"She is . . . well . . . I guess I'll just say to tread lightly. Be careful trusting what she says."

"Really? She always seemed so kind to me," Jacob said. He knew a woman in Holly's profession might be looked askance by a lot of men, but he figured as a fellow business owner Randall must trust her at least enough. "What do you mean?"

Randall's eyes grew cold. "She's poison."

"Holly?" Jacob was surprised out of his normal politeness. "Holly Merritt?"

Randall nodded. "Just be careful. She says she came across the body already stabbed, but how do we know that? She claims to have been so shaken up that she had to retire for the rest of the night, but that just so happened to get her out of talking to you fine gentleman."

"That's true," Lowry said.

"I'm just saying," Randall continued. "Be careful with her."

"Right. Thanks for the warning," Lowry said, nodding. "We actually have a couple questions for you too."

"Oh!" The saloon owner looked surprised. "Let me send someone up to fetch Ms. Merritt for you first." He had a quiet conversation with Buddy before turning back to the lawman.

"You sure you wouldn't like to go back to your office for this?" Jacob asked. He was getting the impression that Randall wasn't taking this seriously as a murder investigation.

"No, no. Here is fine. What else can I help you with?"

Deputy Lowry pulled the bulletin out of his inner pocket, unfolded it, and smoothed it out onto the bar in front of Randall. Jacob kept his eyes fixed on the saloon proprietor, gauging his reaction. Earl Pelling's dark eyes stared out at them from the portrait. It was so true to life, so exactly the same hair, the same jaw of the outlaw that Jacob had spied just a few hours earlier. Randall peered at it.

"Can you tell us about this man?" Lowry asked.

"Well, yes. He does look familiar," Randall said. "I believe he was here a few times in the last few days. Not sure I caught his name before now, though."

"Did you see him with Timson at all?"

Randall nodded slowly. "Maybe once."

"Well—"

Jacob elbowed the deputy before he could continue. He didn't take his eyes off of Randall; the man began biting his nails. They needed to let him fill the silence instead of pressing him with more questions.

Randall stared at the poster in silence for several more moments before looking up. While they were waiting for the saloon proprietor to speak, Deputy Lowry rolled and lit himself another cigarette.

Finally, the man said, "It was only once that I noticed, but I saw Timson spill beer on this man a few days ago. I think it was an accident. I'm almost sure it was an accident. I don't think he meant anything. It was fine." He started to speak faster. "It was just a little thing. An accident."

He lapsed into silence. Lowry and Jacob exchanged a glance.

"Do you know where we could find him?" Jacob asked.

"No. No. Sorry. I didn't even know his name until you showed me . . ." Randall gestured. "But, as I said, I'm sure it was nothing. You're much better off talking to Holly."

"Hello, Deputy."

Jacob turned to see Holly Merritt standing at the foot of the stairs. She wore a navy-blue gown, with her hair done in the same style he had seen last night. Around her otherwise bare shoulders, she had pulled a lace shawl tightly around her, put together primly and carefully for the Sunday morning.

"I understand you wanted to speak to me about what I saw?" She swallowed nervously.

Jacob stood from the barstool to greet her.

"Thank you for meeting us, Ms. Merritt," he said.

"You've been very helpful, Mr. Hall," Lowry said. "Appreciate your time."

"You, um . . ." Randall's eyes darted from one man to the other. "You need anything more from me?" He seemed reluctant to leave them alone.

"We're fine," Lowry said firmly.

"All right. I'll just . . . I'll leave you to it, then."

He looked back over his shoulder as he crossed the room to return to his office. Buddy, the bartender, remained far enough away, cleaning glasses, plausibly out of earshot, but Jacob knew better. Randall had seemed more than a little interested in the investigation and would no doubt have tasked Buddy with keeping an eye on them.

"I apologize we don't have a better space for you, Ms. Merritt," Jacob said. "We would have liked to do this more privately. Please understand we're moving quickly and solving the murder must be the priority."

"Of course."

"Have a seat. Can I get you anything to drink?"

"Oh, no, thank you, Mr. Payne. That's very thoughtful of you."

As she sat, she looked frailer than Jacob had ever seen her, pale and delicate, and he wondered if she had gotten any sleep at all the previous night.

"You claim to have found Mr. Timson's body, do you not?" Lowry asked abruptly.

She seemed to shrink into herself. "Yes, that's right."

"You don't think it is awfully convenient that you were seen earlier this week handling the murder weapon and then just happened to be the only person upstairs when the man died?"

"What . . . ? No, I wasn't—"

"You expect us to believe that you weren't there when the man died? That you just happened upon the body?"

"Well, yes, I do. It's the truth."

"That is for us to decide, Ms. Merritt."

"Ask me whatever you like. I have nothing to hide."

"I'm glad to hear that," Lowry said, standing. "Because before we get to any more questions, Mr. Payne and I will be searching your room."

Jacob looked at the deputy, surprised. He figured this would be necessary but didn't realize it would be their first step.

"What? No. I can't have my privacy violated in this way," Holly protested. She stood and positioned herself between the lawman and the foot of the stairs.

Lowry was firm. "We have to, Ms. Merritt. Step aside, please."

CHAPTER EIGHT

Holly Merritt continued to voice her protests, following closely behind Jacob and Deputy Lowry as they headed up the stairs to her private quarters at the Golden Saddle Saloon. She must have been making quite a racket; Jacob noticed by the time they reached the second floor that Randall Hall had joined their party as well. All along the hallway, girls still in robes poked their pin-curled heads out of doors to see what the noise was. Jacob tried to calm the woman, but she was furious.

"You have no right," she claimed again. "There is no reason you have to search my room. This is . . . this is an outrage!"

"If you really have nothing to hide, Ms. Merritt," Lowry said without looking around, "I would think you would have no objection to us taking a look."

Jacob had forgotten how pompous the deputy could be during an investigation. He seemed to be more aggressive the less sure he was about something. He had lit himself another cigarette, letting slip his nervousness. Jacob would be the first to admit their evidence against Holly wasn't anywhere close to damning, but merely circumstantial. But this was Lowry's show, he reminded himself.

At the end of the hallway they reached the door to Holly's apartment suite. Lowry tried the door and found it locked. He turned to glare at Holly, who sneered back at him.

"Unlock this right now."

"I won't."

"Come on, Holly." Randall put his hand on her arm and tried to speak to her gently. "They need to take a look. If you don't unlock it for them, I will have to."

"Some friend you are," she said. She rolled her eyes and drew out from the neckline of her gown a long necklace with a key on the end. "You boys aren't going in there on your own. I won't stand for that. I'll be standing right there the whole time."

"That's fair, Ms. Merritt." Jacob tried to be

soothing as she handed the key over to Lowry, but he could tell the woman wasn't even listening to him.

When the door swung open, the men were treated to something none of them had experienced in quite a while: the delicate scent of lavender and clean linens. Holly Merritt's private quarters were divided into a small living area and an even smaller bedroom to the right. She had a tidy vanity, a wash stand, two chairs, and a cozy settee to welcome any guests she might have in her sitting area. Jacob could imagine Holly welcoming one of her girls in to talk, drink tea, and help solve their problems. After all, that's what a good madam did: she played surrogate mother to these younger women who were far from home and what they had grown up with.

Lowry was already deep into the room, going through the containers of powder, perfume, and jewelry on the vanity. Jacob took a step inside and peered into the bedroom. The patchwork quilt on the narrow bed was clean and smooth. The curtains were worn, but heavy and fine. There was even a vase of fresh wildflowers on the bedside table. Jacob was loathe to disturb anything in this neat chamber, but he knew they had to search.

"Be careful with that!"

The knocking sounds of drawers being opened and dug through carried on behind him while Jacob walked farther into the private bedchambers. Some silk and lace and delicate clothing hung on hooks to the left of the door. He gently pushed the fabric aside, checking for something hidden underneath, but found nothing. He dropped to his knees to check under the bed and again found it clean and bare. Not even a loose bobby pin had found its way to that clear surface. The bedside table was merely that; no drawer or hidden compartment existed to hide any clue or detail tying Holly to the death of Bob Timson.

That left only the large wardrobe in the corner for Jacob to search.

It pained Jacob to be going through a woman's private, personal space, but the law was the law. If Deputy Lowry thought they had sufficient reason to suspect Holly Merritt, Jacob needed to do his part to bring the dead man justice.

He opened both doors of the wardrobe and peered inside. Like the rest of her apartment, this too was neat, clean, and well organized. If she had hidden any clue from the night before,

Holly was thorough and deliberate about it. Not a single stocking looked out of place.

The murmurs of conversation carried on in the sitting room; it seemed evident that Lowry had not yet found anything of note.

Jacob self-consciously wiped his hands on his shirt before reaching into the wardrobe. He ran his hand along the inside wooden panel, first on one side and then the other, looking for a gap or button that indicated a hidden panel or compartment. He took the linens and boxes out of the floor of the wardrobe and performed the same check along the bottom. Everything appeared to be exactly as it seemed, simply a well-loved piece of furniture that held the whole of Ms. Merritt's life.

Though he couldn't hear all of what was being said, the conversation in the sitting room seemed to be getting heated. Perhaps Lowry had found something, or perhaps he had run out of places to search. Whichever the case, it sounded as though Holly was not going to succumb quietly.

Jacob pulled out the first of the hatboxes that rested on the top shelf of the wardrobe and opened it cautiously. Inside was a flowered straw hat with one large hatpin speared through it. Jacob smiled, thinking about what occasion Holly would have to wear such a contraption.

As he replaced the lid of the hatbox and moved to return it to its place, he heard something heavy slide inside and the weight of the box shift as he tilted it. There must be something else within. He set the lid to the box aside and carefully lifted the hat with one hand.

There, sitting in the center of the hatbox previously disguised by the hat itself, was a thick folded and bound stack of greenbacks. Even with just a glance, Jacob guessed it must be close to a thousand dollars.

Timson had been widely known in the short time he was in Tucson to be carrying large amounts of cash.

Jacob's heart began beating more quickly.

He left the hat and box on Holly's bed and carried the wad of bills into the sitting room, held out in front of him like a weapon.

"I appreciate that you're trying to help, Randall, but—" Lowry was saying. He stopped short when he spotted Jacob. "What is that?" He spoke quietly, cautiously, as though Jacob were carrying a rattlesnake he didn't want to spook.

"Can you tell us about this, Ms. Merritt?" Jacob asked, still holding the cash gingerly.

She opened her mouth, but then closed it again without a sound. She shook her head and collapsed onto her settee, drawing her shawl more closely around her.

"This seems like an awful lot of money for someone in your profession to be holding," Jacob suggested.

"It's not," she said. "I mean, it *is*. That's true. But I've been saving for such a long time. It's all mine. It's—"

"Where did you get all that money?" Randall asked.

Jacob frowned at him. Randall's input wasn't helping. He handed the evidence he had discovered to the deputy and then took hold of Randall's arm.

"We appreciate your help, Mr. Hall, but we need to conduct this interview in private. Ms. Merritt deserves that."

"Oh, I see," Randall said. "Of course. I'll just . . . I'll wait in the hallway, shall I?"

"Better to wait down in your office. We can find you there if we have questions."

"All right." He nodded. "I'm happy to help."

Jacob nodded back, lips pursed, and closed the door to Holly's quarters, shutting the other man out. When he turned around, Lowry was scowling at their suspect, who sat slumped with her head in her hands.

"Did you steal this money from Timson, Ms. Merritt? Is that why you were in his room last night? To take advantage of the poor man?"

"No!" she all but shouted. She caught herself and took a deep breath before continuing. "No. I told you. The money is mine. Not only am I quite good at my job, but I am responsible as well. I've been saving every penny I could for a long time."

"Look around," Lowry said angrily. "You have possibly the nicest room in all of Tucson. You expect me to believe you haven't been spending your money on all this fine linen and jewelry?"

"None of this is luxurious or irresponsible, Deputy. If you were smart about how you spent your money and didn't squander every night drinking and gambling, maybe you too could have nice things."

Jacob winced. The deputy was already acting as though his pride had been wounded; further criticism would not help her case.

"Believe me or don't believe me," she continued. "I don't know what else I can say to convince you of the truth. That money is mine, earned fairly, and you're wasting your time here.

Have you even looked into what Lucky and Abe were doing last night? I heard the argument between them and Timson. I would have thought you'd begin there."

"We have lots of tips we are following," Jacob said. "But since you brought it up, what else can you tell us about Lucky and Abe?"

"I know they're not making themselves any friends. It seems as though every man I talk to has lost money to them."

"Including me," Lowry said.

Holly laughed. "Sorry. I could have warned you not to play with them."

Jacob waved his hand to deflect. "Serves him right. But those men taking money in card games is not the same as them murdering an unsuspecting victim."

"That's true. But you know as well as I do that plenty of damage can be done in the name of self-defense. That fight we witnessed last night was not the first."

"Oh?" Lowry asked, leaning forward.

She shook her head. "I believe that was at least the third time I saw Mr. Timson confront Lucky and Abe in the last week. In fact, after the second time, a couple days ago, I overheard those boys talking about leaving town."

"What did they say?" asked Jacob. "Did they

realize you could hear them?"

She shrugged. "A woman in my line of business knows plenty of secrets. I hear a lot of things. Most men don't pay any attention to whether or not I'm listening."

"Did they say when they were leaving?"

"No, but I got the impression that it would be soon. I wouldn't be at all surprised if this murder investigation pushed up their timeline."

"We've got to find them," Lowry said. "Now. Today. We've got to question them."

"At least Lucky. He disappeared well before Abe. We don't know where he went," Jacob said. "I remember thinking it strange he'd leave Abe behind, since I've never seen them apart."

The deputy seemed to be hedging, indecisive about what the next step should be. His hands shook as he lit another cigarette.

"Why don't you go find Lucky and Abe to interview them," Jacob said. "I can stay here with Holly. I'm sure she has more to tell us, but those card-playing boys will respond better to your badge."

Lowry nodded, but still eyed Holly suspiciously. "You're right. I'll be back as soon as I can."

The deputy closed the door behind him, leaving Jacob and Holly alone.

CHAPTER NINE

The day was getting away from them, the number of suspects and threads to follow becoming too much for Jacob and Deputy Lowry to do together. Splitting up to continue the investigation was the only way they could be sure to find the murderer before it was too late.

"Would you like me to open the door, Ms. Merritt? I wouldn't want anyone thinking anything untoward was going on."

She laughed lightly. "Mr. Payne. Being behind a closed door with a single man cannot possibly damage my reputation. I appreciate the offer, but no. I would rather this conversation take place in private. Particularly away from Randall Hall."

That last sentence was so imbued with venom that Jacob was surprised—although, given the warning he had received, maybe he shouldn't be.

"Why Mr. Hall specifically?"

She sat back against the settee and waved her hands impatiently. "He is just a nuisance sometimes. He already knows more than he should and I don't trust him."

Before asking any more questions, Jacob watched her for a moment. Though she seemed a little overwhelmed by the events of the morning thus far, she didn't give away any sign or indication that she was deceiving him or hiding anything. Holly drew a plain white handkerchief from the end of her sleeve and dabbed at her forehead, wiping away the sheen of sweat from her heated exchange with Deputy Lowry.

"Tell me more about why you don't trust Mr. Hall."

She looked at him in surprise. Jacob supposed she had expected his line of questioning to be about her and her activities, but he suspected she had plenty of information on a range of topics that might be helpful. After a moment, he realized she was scrutinizing him. Holly took a long, hard look at him, likely deciding whether or not he was trustworthy as well.

After a while she said, "It's difficult to describe. Maybe it's just my woman's intuition, but there's something about him. I always feel as though he is trying to manipulate me into doing what he wants."

"How long have you been here?"

"At the Golden Saddle? Oh, I think coming up on five years now? I came out west right after the war ended. I couldn't stand to see the places I loved as a girl so changed, and in some cases destroyed. I wanted a fresh start."

She paused. "But Randall wasn't here then. He only bought the business in the last year. Right before you arrived in Tucson, I think."

Jacob grunted. "That means that any statement he makes about your income, or ability to save money, is only based on the last year?"

She nodded. "I want to believe he means well, Jacob, but . . ."

"I see."

His brain was whirring. Whatever was going on between Randall and Holly, whatever reason one had to warn about the other, whatever actually happened in Timson's room last night when either or both of them came upon the body,

Jacob knew for a fact he was not being told everything.

"Tell me, Ms. Merritt, do you know how Randall might feel about you? Does he know you don't trust him?"

"Oh!" She laughed. "Possibly. But also I wouldn't be surprised if he doesn't pay attention to anyone outside of himself. I would say I am pleasant to him, but not warm."

"I see. I think I understand. I want to ask you about the wad of cash I found."

Her face fell.

"Even if I believe that it is all rightfully yours," he continued, "what am I to think about that? What will you even do with such a sum?"

"What does anyone do with money saved?" she retorted. "I aim to make a better life for myself. I don't want to live in dusty, tiny Tucson forever, and I certainly don't want to run a bordello until I'm old. That money you found is my retirement. That sum is almost enough to get out of here and set me up for the rest of my life. I may take up sewing, or even teaching if I can, but as soon as I leave Tucson, I'm leaving this life behind me."

"That's very admirable. Did Randall know about this plan?"

She scoffed. "He wasn't happy about it, I'll

tell you. As soon as he took over the business, I told him confidentially that I wouldn't be staying much longer. He didn't take the news well. Seemed to think I owed him and that he was somehow a victim because I was taking charge of my own life."

"I'm sorry," Jacob said.

"Oh, thank you, but I'm used to it. Ever since then, though, he's always giving me snide comments about how he hopes I fail and knows that I'll regret leaving. That man is bitter about something, but I don't aim to stick around and figure out what."

"When will you leave?"

"I was planning on after the first of the year. But with all this"—she gestured to him—"I'm thinking as soon as possible might be better for me."

"Ms. Merritt, you know we can't let you leave Tucson as long as you're under suspicion of murder."

"Am I, then?" She sighed and leaned back into her seat. "You hadn't said. Well . . ."

"I'm sure you understand," Jacob said gently.

"Yes. All right. Very well. Of course I understand." She sighed again and sat up straight. "I'm sure you have more questions for me, don't you, Mr. Payne?"

The new coldness in her voice made him cautious.

"Yes, thank you. Let's go back to your movements last night. I saw you downstairs—"

"At the same time Lucky and Abe were arguing with Mr. Timson, yes. I remember."

"—and then you left, specifically telling us you were going to speak to Timson. Did you come right upstairs? Can you retrace your movements from last night?"

Holly examined her nails as she thought.

"Who does Lowry think did it?" she asked abruptly.

"I . . . I really don't think I should talk about the investigation."

"Of course. I understand. I was just wondering if there's a reason he left you here to watch over me instead of taking you with him."

"I couldn't say, ma'am. Could we get back to the question at hand, though? Can you tell me about what you did last night?"

"Well, let me think. After I witnessed Mr. Timson anger at least two people, I checked in on two of my girls who were near the bar. They had been feeling poorly yesterday afternoon and I had told them I would give them the night off if they needed it."

"What were their names? In case we need to verify this."

Holly took a deep breath and closed her eyes, calming herself. "It was Tabitha and Louise. They'll confirm."

"And how long did you talk to them?"

"Oh, not long. Fewer than ten minutes."

"And then you went upstairs?"

"No, then I went behind the bar to get myself a drink."

"Mr. Hall allows that?"

She smirked. "Mr. Hall doesn't know everything that happens here."

"Okay." Jacob smiled. "And how long did it take you to do that?"

"A minute or two. Not long. Then I went upstairs. I think maybe one or two men stopped to chat with me on my way."

"Shall we say a delay of another minute or two?"

"Better call it five minutes, with all the stops. I can't afford to be short with any of them, have to at least make them feel like I've paid attention to them."

Jacob bowed his head in understanding. "Very good. Another five minutes. Then you were upstairs."

"Right."

"And is it at that point that you found Mr. Timson?"

She paled and nodded. "When I got to the top of the stairs, I could see that his door was open just a tiny bit. Whoever had . . ." She paused and closed her eyes, taking several deep breaths before continuing. "Whoever had killed him"—her voice broke—"had not closed the door behind them completely. I thought I would just pop my head in and say hello, you know? He's one of our biggest— That is, he *was* one of our biggest clients for the last week. I thought I'd be a good hostess and check up on him."

"Did you hear anything?"

"I . . . no, I don't think so." Holly looked thoughtful. "Although, now that you mention it, I might have heard some floorboards farther down the hallway creak, but I couldn't be sure. I was a bit distracted, I'm sure you understand."

"Of course."

"And it could have been any number of people on a Saturday night up in the cribs."

"I understand."

"So, I walked up to Mr. Timson's door and I knocked. I thought I heard something, so I pushed the door open the rest of the way, and then . . . well, you know."

Jacob nodded. Her screams had been heard throughout the entire saloon.

"You didn't touch anything when you were in there? You didn't see anything out of place or suspicious?"

She gave him an exasperated look. "You mean other than seeing a man lying bleeding all over the floor? No, Mr. Payne. I did not."

"I see."

Jacob paused to think, and Holly allowed them to sit in silence while he did. The question came down to whether or not he believed this woman. Was this money her longtime savings, or was it perhaps a recent acquisition? Is this murder of financial gain or was she simply the unlucky one to discover a body?

Jacob looked at Holly, who had bowed her head and clasped her hands. He decided then and there that he did trust her. He did believe her. Given both of their behaviors, he had more reason to doubt Randall's story than he did hers, and—provided she cooperated—he was prepared to tell Lowry as much.

"Is there anything else about last night you think we should know, Ms. Merritt?"

"No. No, I think that's everything. I'm a little ashamed of myself now. I don't know how long I stood there screaming before Randall found me. It didn't seem like long at all, but then, I was probably in shock. I'm so sorry I couldn't find the strength to speak to you last night."

"It's fine. Really. We understand. Coming across a sight like that must have been quite a shock."

She nodded, and breathed out hard, as though holding back tears.

"I need you to do something for me," Jacob continued. "Can you promise to stay in town until this is sorted? I will speak to Lowry about you—I think we can drop you from our suspects list. But I need to know you're not going to run. I need to know I can trust you."

"Of course," she said, almost looking offended. "I have nothing to hide. I have no intention of leaving under a cloud of suspicion. Tell Deputy Lowry I'm happy to answer any questions he has as well."

"Tell me what?"

The door swung open quickly to reveal the deputy in the doorway, having only caught the very last bit of her speech.

"You're staying here, Ms. Merritt," the deputy continued. "In fact, to ensure you stay here, I have a mind to arrest you."

"What happened with Abe and Lucky?"

Jacob asked, standing to greet the deputy.

He snorted derisively. "Couldn't even find Lucky. Abe claims he was out grabbing a meal, but I suspect he saw me coming and ran. I told Abe what I thought about him, though."

Jacob winced. "You told Abe that his gambling partner was under suspicion for murder?"

"Not in so many words. I told him we wanted to speak to him. Abe said he'd deliver the message. We ought to go back there later today. But what is it Ms. Merritt needed to tell me?"

Holly sat up straighter. "I just told Mr. Payne I'd answer whatever questions you have. I have nothing to hide."

"Good. Why don't you come with me to the jail to get started?"

Lowry moved to grab the woman's arm, but Jacob stopped him.

"Hold on, Deputy. I've heard what she has to say, and I think we're on the wrong track."

Lowry gave him a doubtful look. "You believe her story about the money?"

"I do. And I also believe that she won't leave town until the murder is solved."

Lowry glanced at Holly, still doubtful. "Can we really believe a woman in her profession?"

"I do," Jacob said quietly. "I believe her. I will vouch for her. In fact, if she doesn't keep her promise, you can . . ." He searched for something sufficiently serious. "You can duel me."

Lowry sighed and rolled his eyes. "I don't want to do that, but all right, Payne. We'll leave her be for now. I don't like it, but you're right. We have plenty of other threads to chase down too." He pulled out his pocket watch. "Seems we have another hour or so before church is let out, but I'd be surprised if any of our men were there."

"All right." Jacob nodded. "In the meantime, we should see if we can find Earl Pelling. He could have had access to Timson, and we already know he's a wanted outlaw."

"I won't confine you to your room, Ms. Merritt," the deputy said as they exited. "But I expect to be able to find you any time I choose."

"I understand, Deputy."

With Holly secure, that left only a few more suspects to track down and possibly eliminate. Jacob and Deputy Lowry stepped out of the saloon and into the sunny street and were immediately halted by a confrontational yell.

"Where is she?"

CHAPTER TEN

Still standing on the boardwalk, Jacob spun around toward the accusing voice. Abe and Lucky stormed down the middle of the main street toward the Golden Saddle Saloon. They both glared at the lawmen, each resting a hand threateningly on the handles of their holstered revolvers.

"Where is she?" Lucky roared again. "Holly Merritt, where's she at?"

Jacob flinched. He realized this was the most he had ever heard the man speak outside of the single word he'd uttered last night. Every other interaction he'd had with the man, Abe spoke for both of them. But now, in his anger, Lucky was provoked into speaking. Into yelling.

"What can I help you with?" Lowry asked pompously, lighting a cigarette.

The gamblers closed the distance in just a few more steps, barreling toward where Jacob and the deputy stood.

"Don't give me that horse shit," Abe said, pushing the man back with his fingers. "You told me Holly Merritt was slinging lies about us. About *him*." He nodded toward his partner. "And when I told Lucky what she's been saying, he insisted we come down here and confront her ourselves."

Jacob shot Lowry an incredulous look. Getting one suspect furious at another was surely no way to conduct a murder investigation. The deputy paled, but puffed out his chest defiantly. Jacob could all but see the man's self-doubt creeping in, causing him to make rash decisions.

"I did no such thing," the deputy protested. "I merely stated that some additional information had come to light about Lucky."

"And then you told us you had been interviewing Holly Merritt," Abe said mockingly. "We're not stupid, Deputy. What has that catty minx been saying?"

"Whoa." Jacob could feel his anger rising in his throat. "There's no need for names, gentlemen. Ms. Merritt has been a valuable witness, as we hope you will be as well. Why don't we all calm down?"

He tried to reach out to the gamblers, but Lucky hit his forearm hard, pushing him away. The glare the man shot Jacob was frightening. He may be done speaking again, but he could still communicate his wrath.

"Who keeps yelling my name?" Just behind the deputy, Holly exited the saloon and stood, hands on hips, staring down the angry men. "You boys know perfectly well I'm not afraid of you. Why don't you say what you've come to say?"

Abe took half a step back, but bumped into Lucky and regained his composure. "What did you say about us and that man Timson? I know you've been talking, trying to throw blame. You know we ain't done nothing and then you send the law our way?"

"Oh, heavens." Holly rolled her eyes. "I did nothing of the kind."

Jacob watched this exchange with interest. Was Lucky so angry because the accusation hit home or because he was truly innocent? Did Holly actually believe the gambler could also be a killer, or was she trying to deflect from herself?

"Then why did this fella show up in our room, huh? Why is the deputy bothering us on a Sunday morning when there are plenty of other actual criminals to be chasing after? Hell"—Abe threw up his hands in frustration—"we got a goddamned known bank robber in Tucson and neither of these boys are even paying attention."

"Wait. What did you say?" Jacob asked.

"You've been running your mouth, Holly," Abe continued without acknowledging Jacob. He pushed past Deputy Lowry to wag his finger in the woman's face. Lucky followed close behind, glaring at her over his friend's shoulder. "Don't you tell me otherwise."

"Hey now, boys," the deputy said, wedging his body between them and Holly again. "I can't have you threatening my witness. We're just trying to get the facts, and now that you're here we can ask you too."

"Ms. Merritt," Jacob said quietly. "Why don't you go back inside now? We'll deal with this. Remember what you told me, and we'll come find you if we have further questions."

"All right then," she said. She shot one last glare at the gamblers before turning her back and reentering the saloon.

"Now, gentlemen," Lowry said. "I'm sure you

understand we've got to pursue all avenues. We've got some questions for Lucky about his actions last night, that's all."

"Maybe we should go inside? Find a quiet place?" Jacob suggested.

Lucky was still breathing hard from the furious adrenaline that coursed through him, but he had calmed enough to nod his assent. Jacob led the way into the saloon, where Holly had already disappeared. Buddy showed a small flash of surprise to see four men enter this early on a Sunday morning, but no other employees were present. As he led the way to an empty table, Jacob waved the bartender away.

He pulled out a chair and sat, as around him Lowry and Abe did the same. Lucky, however, seemed too agitated. He pulled out a chair and then pushed it back in again. He walked a lap around the table, tried again before finally deciding to stand behind the chair, arms crossed in front of him, and scowled at Jacob and the deputy.

"You don't want to sit?" Jacob asked. "Might help you relax."

Lucky shook his head and continued his stare.

"All right," Lowry said, taking charge. "As I said, we have heard a report of the two of you getting into an altercation with the deceased and wanted to follow up."

Abe looked at Jacob and then Lucky. "A what?"

"A fight. With Timson," Jacob clarified.

"Oh."

"Our witness says you've argued with him more than once, yesterday and just a couple days ago. Is that true?"

"Well . . ." Abe hedged. "It might be. I'm not sure we remember the man you're talking about. What did you say his name was?"

Jacob wasn't buying it. He leaned forward across the table at Abe. "Timson. Bob Timson. Traveling salesman. Short, stocky man with red hair."

"Timson . . ." Abe said, pretending to think hard about it.

"I literally saw you get into a fight with him just last night. Just before he was murdered, as a matter of fact," Jacob reminded him.

"Oh, that fella!"

Jacob didn't believe for a moment that Abe had only just recognized who they were discussing. "And before last night?"

"Can't say that I recall—"

"Let me remind you we already have one eye-witness and we can likely find more."

"Oh, now I seem to remember. Maybe a few days ago. That's right. It was also about his losses."

"And at the time, did Mr. Timson threaten you?"

Lucky scoffed.

"Course he did," Abe said. "That man threatened nigh on every man in Tucson."

"And yet," Jacob pressed, "just a couple nights later, you played poker with him again?"

Abe shrugged. "The man likes a game. We were some of the few that were still willing to play with him." He added, his voice low, confidential, "He's kind of a sore loser."

"And then, last night," Lowry said, "after you, shall we say, 'relieved' him of his cash, what happened?"

"We left," Abe said, resting his palm flat against his chest. "Anyone will tell you that. I headed out of the saloon and back to our room. I was ready to call it a night. Lucky got there not long after I did."

"And in the intervening minutes, Lucky?" Jacob addressed the silent man, who was now leaning against the wall by his empty chair. "We know you left first. What happened while you two were apart?"

The gambler nodded his head toward the

door of the saloon, or toward the bar, or the stairs. From where they were sitting, Jacob couldn't be positive which the man was indicating.

"Come on, friend," Lowry said gently. "We know you ain't mute. You gotta tell us where you were, or we'll have cause to take you to jail."

Lucky scowled even harder and glanced at Abe. The men shared some nonverbal communication, which ended with Lucky sighing heavily.

"Out," he said. His voice was deep and gravelly, as though rusty from disuse.

"On the way, did you run into anyone?" Jacob asked. "Did anyone see you leave? Did you happen to talk to—or, that is, did anyone talk to you?"

Lucky shook his head.

"So you have no way to prove that this happened the way you claim?"

He shrugged, unperturbed.

Jacob took a slow breath in and rubbed his temple. For as crowded as the saloon was the previous night, how did no one see anything that happened? He looked at Deputy Lowry, who shrugged.

"I got no cause," he said.

Jacob nodded. He knew that was true.

None of their many suspects had actually given them solid reason to arrest them. They'd need to keep digging, keep looking for the one final piece of evidence that made them sure of guilt.

"Can you boys do something for us?" Jacob asked them. The condescending smirk on Abe's face was almost enough to make him swallow his words, but he forged ahead. "I don't know what you all were planning to do next, but can we ask you to stay in town?"

The men exchanged a look.

"We may have more questions for you. Just don't leave Tucson until after we've found the killer," Lowry said.

"And what if you never find him, eh?" Abe said. "Can't say I have much faith in the law of this town, with that bank robber and everything going on right under your noses."

Jacob grasped on that. "Wait. You said something like that earlier. What do you mean? Who should we be looking at?"

"Nope. Nuh-uh." Abe shook his head. "I'm not telling you nothing. There's nothing worth getting on the bad side of any outlaw in this town. I'm not doing your job for you."

Jacob banged his fist on the table; he was through with being patient. "Tell us, Abe. The sooner we get that man in jail, the safer everyone will be. Including you."

There was a short pause before the gambler spoke again. "I'm just telling you to double check your 'wanted' notices." He stood up and moved to stand next to Lucky. "I heard there was a bank robbed in Prescott not too long ago."

The two men were already headed toward the door of the saloon as Jacob called after them. "Stay in town, boys."

Abe lifted a hand to acknowledge he heard, but neither turned around as they left.

"Who—" Jacob began before being interrupted.

A heavy thump sounded from the back of the saloon, from the closed door to Randall's office.

Both Jacob and Lowry jumped to their feet.

"No!" a female voice cried from behind the door.

"Holly," Jacob said, starting toward the office.

Before he could reach it, the door swung open and Holly stumbled out, holding her hand-kerchief to her mouth.

"You are no man," she said vehemently. "How dare you? How *dare* you!"

"Ms. Merritt," Jacob said as he reached her side. "Are you all right?"

"He—" she said, pointing to Randall, who stood in the doorway of his office. "That—that monster struck me!"

"Randall Hall!" Jacob said, shocked. He stood between him and Holly. "How could you?"

"She was . . ." he began, flustered. "Oh, you don't understand. She had it coming."

Jacob had never seen the saloon proprietor so perturbed. Whatever argument the two had been in must have been greatly upsetting to him. Randall had never seemed like the type to get into a physical confrontation with anyone, let alone with a woman.

"What is this about?" Lowry asked, making his way to Randall's side. "Let's talk about this."

"No," Randall said shortly. "It's fine. Never mind. We're fine."

"Holly?" Jacob asked gently.

If she was bothered by his use of her Christian name, she didn't show it. She dabbed at the small cut on her lip. Fortunately the blood was already beginning to dry.

"You catch that killer," she said, talking to Jacob but still glaring at Randall. "Catch that man so I can get out of this blasted town and away from *him*."

CHAPTER ELEVEN

Holly stormed up the stairs to her private room on the second floor. Randall slammed his office door, locking himself alone inside. In the main room of the Golden Saddle Saloon, Jacob and Lowry looked at each other, amazed at what they had just witnessed. Jacob's head was swimming with all the new information, accusations, and additional leads they had heard in the last half hour. It felt like they were getting closer to discovering who had murdered Bob Timson the night before, but every step forward was excruciating.

One glance at Deputy Lowry, however, told Jacob he needed to step up and take charge. The lawman was pale and sweating. As Jacob watched, Lowry collapsed into an empty chair and pulled out his handkerchief to wipe his brow.

"I don't know, Payne," the deputy said. "Men striking women? Us trusting gamblers to do us a favor? I'm not sure what to do next."

"You still got that picture of Earl Pelling?"

Lowry nodded and patted the pocket where the paper was hidden away.

"We already know there's a murderer in town," Jacob said. "We find him and maybe we solve our own murder too."

Five minutes later, Jacob and Deputy Lowry were stepping into the dim interior of Tucson's livery. Caleb Shaw, in the middle of hauling a saddle, seemed surprised to see them.

"Hey there, Deputy," he said slowly, confused. "It's Sunday morning, ain't it? You fixing to go riding?"

"Morning, Caleb. We're looking for a man been hanging around town the last few days. Wondered if you've seen him."

"Of course, happy to help." He put down the saddle that had filled his arms and gestured to a bale of hay sitting just inside the door. "Would you like a seat?"

The contrast between interviewing this witness and interviewing Holly Merritt made Jacob grin to himself. He supposed you never knew what you'd be running into out here in the west.

"What's this man look like?" Caleb asked before taking a swig from his whiskey flask. He generously offered it to the other two, who both declined.

Lowry fished out the folded bulletin and smoothed it out on his knee. Caleb leaned over to look, chewing his lip thoughtfully.

"Hm. I think maybe I have seen him. Earl Pelling, his name is?"

Lowry nodded, looking at him closely. "When did you see him?"

"Oh . . ." Caleb leaned back against the wooden slats and ran his fingers through his whispy hair while he thought. "Must have been three or four days ago now. But I seen him twice in the same day."

Lowry furrowed his brow. "He came back here the same day?"

Caleb nodded. "Showed up not long after dawn, wanting the names of men who might buy a horse. Thought of you right off, Payne"—he nodded to Jacob—"before I remembered you got Blaze from that Mormon fella."

"I appreciate the thought, Caleb," Jacob said.

Lowry pressed the subject. "So you sent him to someone else?"

"Yeah. There's two or three others here right now that might be looking. Larry, I think his name was. Maybe the reverend over at the Baptist church too."

"But then this man Pelling came back later the same day," Lowry confirmed.

"Oh, right," Caleb said, returning to his original thought. "I thought it was strange, as a matter of fact. When he first showed up he was on a horse, asking about selling it, and when he came back he was on foot asking about *buying* a horse. I asked him why he didn't just keep the one he had, but he growled at me."

"He growled at you?" Lowry chuckled. "You never got an answer out of him?"

"Nope. Just had to tell him I didn't know of any horses for sale. You'd think he'd understand, since I gave him three different names of men who were buying, but . . ." Caleb shrugged. "So he left again, and I haven't seen him since."

"You're sure it was this man?" Lowry asked, pointing to the bulletin.

"Yep. Say, there isn't a chance I could get some of that bounty on him, is there?" The eight-hundred-dollar reward was plastered in huge letters above Pelling's face.

"Are you going to go try to capture him?" Lowry asked with a wry smile.

"Oh, no. You're right. That seems like a bad idea, huh?" Caleb grinned sheepishly.

"Did he give you any more info, or any other details about where he'd be? What about this fella you said was looking to buy a horse? Larry?"

Caleb nodded. "Yeah. Wait." He frowned. "No. Not Larry. Lenny? I think Lenny. He's kind of new to town, too, but came here looking to buy."

"Lenny," Jacob repeated. What were the chances it was the same Lenny Duffin they had seized and interviewed the night before? "Any idea where we can find this Lenny?"

Caleb shook his head. "I'll just tell you what I told Earl. Lenny, skinny and tall with dark scraggly hair, and I've seen him most every night at the Golden Saddle. I don't know where to find him otherwise."

"I guess we'll have to go back there," Lowry said, standing, prompting Jacob to do the same. "Feels like we're running around in circles. Caleb, don't tell anyone what we talked about today, will you?"

Caleb held his hands out in placation, grinning again. "No, sir. I don't need any wanted murderer knowing I know something."

"Smart man." Lowry shook his hand and said his goodbyes.

"I have an idea," Lowry said grimly when they were alone again, walking through the streets of Tucson.

The midday sun was creeping overhead, and the churches must have let out because more and more citizens filled the streets. The passage of time reminded Jacob first how hungry he was, but more so how little time they had left to solve this murder while it was still difficult to leave Tucson.

"We need to think," Jacob said. "We need to go over what we've already learned, and I for one need to eat. I'm not sure we can do anything more or make any other decisions right now."

"You just want to go visit Bonnie Loft," Lowry said with a grin.

Jacob laughed in spite of himself. "She might not even be working today," he said. "She's probably not, in fact. It's Sunday."

"Nevertheless," Lowry said, "you're right. Let's eat."

The San Xavier Cafe was only four blocks from where they were, and the short walk gave

Jacob a chance to catch the deputy up with what he had learned from Holly. Lowry was sympathetic to Holly's plight, and her desire to leave Tucson to retire from her current business, but he was far less confident than Jacob as to her innocence. He still insisted they may need to arrest her for the murder.

"We have plenty of cause," Lowry said. "That stack of cash could have been from anything, and most certainly could have been stolen from the missing billfold of that traveling salesman. I'd be hard pressed to find any other man in this town who has that much money readily on hand. Not to mention the fact that we have a witness placing the weapon in her very hand."

"But," Jacob protested, "a witness we later saw hit her in the face."

Lowry shrugged, belligerent. "Maybe she started it. Maybe she tried to attack Randall and he was defending himself."

"It sure didn't look like self-defense to me," Jacob mumbled.

But they had to cut their discussion short as they walked into the cafe and found seats. Jacob was right—Bonnie was not on duty for lunch that day. Instead, a matronly woman Jacob had interacted with only a couple times prior waited on them. The day's special was ham sandwiches with fresh bread and—surprisingly—actual fresh vegetables: sliced sweet peppers. That was one thing about living in the Arizona Territory that Jacob had been looking forward to. With as warm as the weather was, they had two growing seasons; locals had been tantalizing him with promises of greens and fresh fruit for weeks. It looked like that day had finally arrived.

"Thank you, Mrs. Everill," he said when she brought their plates.

"Why, Deputy Lowry! Jacob!"

A familiar face appeared next to the table, and there was Jacob's favorite waitress, Bonnie, dressed in her Sunday best. Both men stood to greet her.

"I didn't expect to see you here on today of all days. I thought you . . ." She dropped her voice to a whisper and looked around. "I would have thought you'd have plenty keeping you busy today."

"Oh, we do," Lowry said. "Lawmen still need to eat, sweetheart."

"What are you doing here?" Jacob asked her, smiling.

"Mrs. Everill sent word that they have peppers today, so I wanted to come have lunch before they ran out. How's the sandwich?" Her eyes looked hungrily at their plates.

"Have a seat," Jacob said, pulling out a chair for her.

"I don't want to intrude . . ."

"Not at all. I insist."

Deputy Lowry tried to catch his eye, but Jacob deliberately didn't look. He needed this. He needed a nice, quiet meal with this amazing woman. The fresh vegetable was just an added bonus. With no new information to impart to the deputy, the two men had hit a dead end of their investigation.

As Bonnie settled herself in the chair, she asked, "How are you, Jacob? What are you two up to today?"

Jacob could tell she was providing them an opening to talk about the investigation without actually asking about it directly. She was always so respectful of what other people needed.

"We're at a bit of a lost, to be honest," he said. "All our threads of investigation have reached an end."

"Oh, that's too bad."

Lowry lit a cigarette as he spoke. "I just don't know what to do next."

"I'm sorry," Bonnie said, commiserating. "I

can't even pretend to understand the way outlaws think. That must be so difficult."

Jacob almost wanted to hug her. Who else would be so understanding?

"Where could they be spending a Sunday, I wonder," she continued. "Your suspects. Not in church, surely?"

"Doesn't seem likely," Jacob agreed.

"Maybe . . . well, as I say, I don't know how criminals think, but it seems like they'll be looking to get out of town, wouldn't you say?"

Jacob paused his chewing. Did she just suggest . . . ?

"I know what our next step is," Jacob said, standing. He threw several dollars down on the table, apologizing to Mrs. Everill and Bonnie for having to leave in such a rush, and led the deputy out of the cafe.

CHAPTER TWELVE

As Jacob approached the livery, he could hear the murmur of conversation within. He held his hand up behind him to slow the deputy and crept up to the door as quietly as possible. Caleb's scratchy tenor voice was evident, though Jacob could only hear every fourth or fifth word. The other voice—or voices—he couldn't identify. It sounded somewhat familiar, but then again, he had heard so many men's voices in his hunts for outlaws that he could be mistaken.

Lowry reached him crouched by the open door, far to the side and out of sight of anyone within.

"Who is that?" the deputy asked in a whisper.

Jacob shook his head. He couldn't be sure

but was growing more and more certain by the second. The group of voices came nearer to the door. He was right. That second voice *was* familiar.

"Sorry, fellas," Jacob heard Caleb say. "I told you. I don't have any extra horses for sale. You're free to hire one for the day or a week, but it has to be tomorrow. I'm not at leave to hire them out today. You'll have to wait until Monday."

"And we told you," an unfamiliar voice growled. "We don't care about no rules or what day it is. You saddle these horses for us now!"

Jacob heard a thud and crash—what sounded like a man's body being pushed into a wooden beam or wall. He cringed, picturing Caleb being attacked by whoever these men were.

"We've got to get in there," Lowry whispered. "Who is that?"

"I'm going around," Jacob whispered back. "I'll try to get high up. Wait for my signal."

Jacob stepped back as the deputy nodded and took his place. Inside, the bullying and fighting continued. He felt bad for Caleb, who had gotten on the bad side of whoever this was —Jacob had suspicions—in spite of his specific effort to mind his own business.

Around the side of the building—toward the shade, so he wouldn't be backlit and silhouetted by the sun—Jacob walked quickly. He scanned the wall, looking for an easy place to climb up. He craned his neck to check the roof. Narrow gaps between the boards let Jacob peer into the dark interior.

Caleb Shaw was scrambling on the ground, backing up against one of the far walls to get away from the man bearing down on him with fist ready. A second man stood to the side, aiming his shotgun at the prone man. When the second man spoke, he turned his body toward where Jacob was watching, giving Jacob a clear view of the man's face behind his dark, scraggly hair.

"Well, he can't do anything if you knock him unconscious, Earl," Lenny said, sneering.

The threatening man with his back to Jacob must be Earl Pelling. His dirty-blond hair peeking out from under his hat matched the description Jacob had seen on the wanted poster.

Bonnie had been right. These men were looking for the fastest way out of Tucson . . . and away from Deputy Lowry's murder investigation.

As the two men moved around Caleb's

vulnerable form, Jacob noticed a square of sunlight cutting through the darkness and onto the dirt floor. He looked up. Somewhere above would be a window or break in the roof. That would be where he needed to climb to. The problem would be doing it quietly enough that the men inside wouldn't hear him through the thin walls.

"Well, look at this," Jacob heard behind him.

He spun around quickly to see Abe and Lucky approaching the livery on his side of the building. Jacob frantically gestured for the men to go away. He couldn't bear to let anyone else come to harm. Caleb was enough, and who knew how many other men had gotten in Earl Pelling's way since he got to Tucson? Bob Timson, for example. Though no fan of the gamblers, Jacob hoped to make it clear that they should leave.

As they continued to stride toward him, Jacob realized they weren't going to take a hint, so he ran the short distance toward them. The better to keep the men inside from hearing the newcomers.

"You can't be here," he whispered. "Lowry is going to make an arrest. You'll just be in the way."

"Oh, really?" Abe grinned and peered

around Jacob to the building. "You boys finally catch up with Lenny Duffin, huh?"

"Yes, we— Wait. Duffin? How do you know it's him in there? We just found him helping out a wanted murderer. Why do you say him?"

Lucky and Abe grinned at each other. The former laughed for the first time since Jacob had known him.

"You serious?" Abe all but shouted.

"Keep your voice down," Jacob warned. "Just spill it."

"You boys just never been to the sheriff's office, I guess?"

"Abe. If you can't be helpful, I'll have to arrest you myself for interfering with an investigation."

"All right, all right," he said, raising his hands in surrender. "I thought you all knew. Lord knows I tried tellin' you earlier. Duffin is a wanted bank robber. Prescott, I think. I heard he's coming through Tucson on his way to Texas with his thousands, but I haven't talked to the man himself."

"Duffin is an outlaw too?"

"Sure is. Why do you say 'too'? Who else is in there?"

"Earl Pelling," Jacob said, watching the gamblers' reactions carefully.

Lucky let out a low whistle.

"Damn, yeah," Abe said. "We heard about that one too."

"Right." Jacob stared at him. "So. Get out of here. You don't want to get hurt."

Lucky was eyeing the building behind Jacob, frowning. He nudged Abe in the arm and indicated with a nod to the front door.

"Really?"

Lucky raised his eyebrows as if in response.

"Fine. Yeah. Okay." Abe turned to Jacob. "We can give you a couple minutes of diversion, but you have got to get to the top of that building as soon as you can."

"What?" Jacob was taken aback.

"We ain't aiming to get killed just for you boys, but we don't want those men in Tucson any more than you do."

Lucky nudged him.

"Oh, yeah," Abe said. "And we want part of the reward."

Jacob grinned in spite of himself. "We'll have to talk to Deputy Lowry about that. Since he'll be the one making the arrest."

"Oh, I reckon that's true." Abe chewed the inside of his cheek. Lucky must have made some indiscernible expression again, because

Abe sighed and said, "Fine. Let's just get this done."

As they headed in one direction, Jacob went in the other, as far away from their promised diversion as possible and ready to scale the wall of the livery to position himself at the window at the top. He looked back at Abe and Lucky several times until they moved around the corner of the building and out of sight. He wished he could have some more control over this situation, some way of guiding how the whole thing played out. Jacob trusted the other men, to an extent, but there were still far too many factors, far too many ways this could fall apart.

When the conversation started up again, on the opposite side of the building near the door, Jacob hesitated only a moment before he began to climb up the side. There were enough gaps and crooked boards to give him purchase, and he was on the roof of the livery in moments.

The shouting grew louder, and Jacob thought he might have heard the crack of a punch. His heart hammered as he edged his way gingerly across the roof to the hay loft that peaked in the middle. Small, square windows peppered the side of it—too small for Jacob to squeeze through, but hopefully big enough for him to keep watch and shoot if he needed to.

He sidled his way to the closest window and peered in. From this angle all he could see was the front door of the livery, but all the men had already moved farther inside the structure. Jacob scooted to the next window over, closer to the middle of the livery, and looked down.

Lowry was nowhere in sight; he must still be waiting by the door, hidden from the men. But Abe and Lucky had either charmed or threatened their way deeper into the livery. Caleb was on his feet now, but still with his back to the wall, shrinking down as though trying not to draw attention. Lucky held his revolver loosely, unholstered but pointed at the ground.

Jacob pressed on the corner of the window. He pulled at the frame. He tried to dig his fingers in and slide the glass to the side, but it didn't budge. He cursed under his breath. It frustrated him that he couldn't hear what was going on in there. He couldn't even take proper aim from this position. If the situation escalated—*when* the situation escalated—he could only guess based on body language. And even then, even assuming his guess was correct, Jacob would only be able to shoot through the glass.

The yelling from inside was growing louder,

but the words were still unintelligible. He glanced down and realized Caleb had disappeared altogether, probably while Jacob was fumbling with the window. He scanned the visible area and prayed the boy had found an opportunity to get far out of the way. With Abe and Lucky providing the diversion, it was possible.

Duffin was now in Lucky's face, shouting as the gambler remained stony faced and mute. From this angle, Jacob could see Lucky's revolver poking right into the other man's ribs, but either he didn't notice or didn't care. Was Duffin bold enough to call Lucky's bluff? Would Abe and Lucky be willing to take the confrontation that far?

Pelling moved to separate the other two men. Jacob wondered at that, and tried to imagine what he was saying. A wanted murderer on the run . . . playing the peacemaker? But as he put his hand on the silent gambler, Lucky shifted his weight, threw up a hand, grabbed Pelling's wrist, and twisted his arm behind his back.

All at once, several things occurred.

A gunshot rang out. Jacob threw his elbow into the glass pane, breaking it, and used a closed fist to get rid of the extra shards of glass.

He barely felt the sharp edges puncture his skin as he took aim and fired.

He hadn't seen where the first bullet landed, but Jacob's own shot took out Duffin in the calf. The outlaw collapsed, grabbing his leg and cursing. Another shot sounded. Jacob guessed Duffin was defending himself, though he didn't know where the bullet had come from. Lucky and Pelling were wrestling, the latter trying to throw off the grip of the former.

Lucky collapsed to the ground and Abe appeared in view, pushing Pelling aside. Jacob kept his gun trained on the murderer, silently begging him to stay down.

But the man didn't listen. Pelling swept his leg toward Abe, knocking the man over. Jacob took aim and fired. As the bullet sank into his bicep, the man cried out angrily.

With the outlaws thus debilitated, Lowry pounced. He came through the door with guns blazing, shouting instructions and barreling his way over to the men.

"Stay down, you bastards," the deputy shouted.

CHAPTER THIRTEEN

"Jacob Payne, get down here now!"

Lowry kept his guns trained on Pelling and Duffin. He glanced up to the broken window briefly before immediately looking back to the outlaws. Next to him, Abe scrambled to his feet and joined the deputy in also training a revolver on one of the outlaws.

Jacob didn't stay at the broken window to see any more. He slid down the incline of the roof to the edge, almost falling off before he regained his grip, turned around, and began the climb down. He dropped the final six feet. When he landed he jarred one ankle, but he didn't let that stop him from running around the building to the front door.

"I'm here," he gasped out, bursting inside.

Lucky had scooted over to lean against one of the stalls, tending to the gunshot in his leg. The two injured outlaws remained on the ground in the center of the open space, guns trained on them. In the back, Jacob could hear Caleb soothing and comforting the horses.

"You two are under arrest," Lowry was saying. "Good, Jacob. Come here. Keep your eye on these men while I cuff them."

Jacob was already halfway across to the deputy. He unholstered his second revolver and pointed both guns at the outlaws. Earl Pelling and Lenny Duffin cast dirty looks at their captors. Which of them had been Timson's murderer? Maybe both. It was clear to Jacob they were working together in something, at least.

"We're going to get you boys a nice cozy spot in the Tucson jail," Lowry said. "I know you've both got warm welcomes waiting for you in other cities. Prescott and Albuquerque, right? We'll be sure to get you back there where you belong."

Through this short monologue, Lowry managed to detain Duffin and Pelling. It helped that the deputy was at least thirty pounds heavier than both men; when one struggled out of his grasp, Lowry simply leaned into it.

"You seem to have this under control," Abe said, holstering his gun. "We're out of here." He helped Lucky to his feet.

The silent gambler nodded at Jacob. The bounty hunter was impressed at the man's uncomplaining demeanor. Maybe a bullet wound was no big deal to him.

For the first time, Jacob had to begrudgingly admire the two men. They had stepped up when they didn't have to. They had helped the law with potentially no reward to them. And they had done it both uncomplainingly and while getting injured. Maybe it wouldn't be so bad if they stayed in Tucson.

Between him and the deputy, they got the two outlaws transported to the jail and imprisoned in separate jail cells. The verbal abuse and harassment Pelling and Duffin spewed were somewhat impressive, though Jacob winced at such language on a Sunday of all days.

"Since you're in custody anyway, one of you might as well confess to last night's murder," Jacob said.

Pelling spat at him, just missing Jacob's boots.

"Really?" Jacob said, contemptuously.

"I didn't do nothin' last night."

"Me either," Duffin chimed in. "I already told you that."

"You must have done something," Jacob said to Pelling. He leaned against the man's cell door, speaking through the bars. "I saw blood on your shirt. You expect me to believe a wanted murderer with blood on him had nothing to do with a murder that very night in the same building I saw you? Do you think I'm stupid, Earl?"

He shrugged. "Apparently you boys didn't realize who this jackass was," he said, gesturing to Duffin. "Y'all seem pretty stupid to me."

Jacob's temper flared. Even someone pointing out what he had missed infuriated him. He was hard enough on himself; he didn't need anyone else piling on.

"Explain the blood, then. If you can't, it'll be damn easy to pin Timson's murder on you."

"Okay. I might have done *some*thing," he conceded. "But not what you think. Nothing even illegal." He grinned, showing Jacob that he was missing at least three teeth. "Truth be told, I had a hankering for a steak. Made my way back to the kitchen and made myself one."

"You—" Jacob paused, flabbergasted. "You just . . . you what? You stole a steak and cooked it yourself?"

"Yep."

Jacob wasn't sure what question to ask next. "And the blood?"

"It was raw when I picked it up," Earl said condescendingly. "I got some of that on my hand."

Jacob winced in disgust. "And you just wiped it on your shirt?"

"Yep." Earl leaned back against the wall of his cell and closed his eyes. "Didn't hurt me none."

"A little steak blood on your shirt could hurt you a lot," Jacob said, "if the deputy thinks it's enough evidence to get you for Timson's murder."

"Nah. You law boys always do the right thing. I know you'll go talk to the bartender at the saloon or whoever you need to to confirm my story. It's . . . what's that word? Them's my *alibi*."

Jacob sighed. He was right. And in spite of Duffin being a wanted outlaw, they still didn't have any additional evidence tying either of these men to Timson's murder.

He was starting to get a headache. The day was getting away from them and the unfortunate salesman may not get the justice he deserved.

Before he could continue with his questioning of the two, the door at the front of the office opened and Jacob overheard someone talking to Lowry. As he got closer to the office, Jacob recognized the voice of Randall, raised and arguing with the deputy.

"You've got to get this taken care of," Randall was insisting. "Arrest her. I told you she had the weapon. You don't think it's a little bit suspicious that Holly Merritt was the first person to find the body? And then you found a stack of money in her room. I'm telling you, I can't have a murderer in my saloon. Arrest her!"

"Calm down, Mr. Hall," Lowry said. "We're close to making an arrest. We just captured two wanted outlaws—"

"That doesn't matter! It was her. *Her!*"

"The men in the cells—"

As Jacob entered the office, the deputy caught his eye, and the bounty hunter subtly shook his head. He couldn't be sure of the men's guilt. They shouldn't be promising Randall anything.

"I'm going to have to ask you to continue to be patient, Mr. Hall," Lowry finished. "We'll get to the bottom of this, arrest the murderer, and then the Golden Saddle Saloon can continue with business as usual."

The man blanched at that promise. "Yes, well. Get to it," he retorted. He slammed his fist on the desk and left the office in a huff.

Jacob followed Randall to the door and watched him walk away, out into the road, pushing past a couple striding slowly. Leaning against the doorframe, Jacob wondered if he should follow the other man. Randall seemed angry and possibly dangerous. Irrational at the very least. There was something off about him, something that made Jacob wonder if he was hiding something.

As Jacob watched, another person turned the corner onto this street. In an instant he recognized it as Holly Merritt and saw that Randall's trajectory was headed straight toward her. In his anger and frustration, Randall didn't seem to be watching where he was going. The bounty hunter instinctively headed toward the impact he knew was coming, if only to mediate and buffer the confrontation before anything got worse.

He hurried his steps. Jacob saw the look of recognition in Holly's eyes, but rather than step aside, out of Randall's way, she simply stopped. Frozen. Possibly too surprised or shocked to make the choice to move. What happened next was not any more easy to watch knowing it was going to happen.

Still with his head down, Randall barreled full into Holly's frozen form. His shoulder rammed into her bosom; Holly put both hands up to protect herself, but the man didn't stop. Jacob was still a dozen steps away when Randall finally looked up to see who he had run into. Though only able to see the back of him, Jacob noticed Randall's neck flush, as though another wave of fury had overtaken him.

"You meddling whore!" Randall shouted at Holly. "Get the hell out of my way!"

Holly shrank back at such an exclamation, paling visibly, but only for a moment before gathering her dignity and defending herself.

"How dare you!" she exclaimed, standing up straight in the face of his wagging, accusing finger. "You can't speak to me that way. You were negligent and sloppy and weren't paying attention."

Jacob reached them in that moment, placing his large hand on Randall's arm and trying to calm the man before he did anything he might regret.

The saloon proprietor threw off the grip angrily, turning to shout at Jacob next.

"Get your hands off me, you worthless

excuse for a man. I'm tired of being the only one who gets anything done around here. The only one who sees what is really happening."

"Now, Mr. Hall—"

"Shut the hell up!" Now his accusing finger was in Jacob's face. "Both of you." He turned back to Holly. "Get out of my way, I said!" With that growl, Randall raised his hands to push Holly physically out of his way.

Jacob Payne had never stood for anyone assaulting a woman in his presence and was not about to give this man a pass for any reason, angry or not. Still mostly behind Randall, Jacob grabbed the other man by the shoulders and yanked him back. The other man lost his balance, his ankles twisting and his feet sliding from underneath him.

He frantically grabbed at both Holly and Jacob to regain his footing, but Holly had already taken two steps back to avoid the shove she had thought coming. As Randall grasped for Jacob, their arms became entangled, wrapped around each other. The man continued to fall, but Jacob's hold on his jacket tore the piece of clothing clean off of him, scattering the matches, billfold, and other items that had been in Randall's pockets.

Jacob let go; Randall sprawled into the dirt,

groaning in pain and surrounded by the detritus of his life.

"I didn't want to have to do that," Jacob said sternly. "You owe Ms. Merritt an apology. Let me—"

Just as Jacob was about to help Randall to his feet, he recognized the billfold, delicately embroidered with a red rose, that lay in the dirt.

CHAPTER FOURTEEN

Jacob had almost looked away. He had almost helped the other man to his feet and apologized. He had even almost moved on, leaving Randall to his privacy. But something tickled his brain. That embroidered red rose . . .

"Dang it," Randall whispered to himself as he followed Jacob's gaze and tried to sweep up the billfold.

"No," the bounty hunter said darkly. He stepped on Randall's outstretched wrist, halting his reach for the billfold. "I'll take that."

As soon as the decorated billfold was in his hand, Jacob knew it was familiar. He knew he had seen it before. He and the deputy had been looking for this very item. Jacob unfolded the worn leather gingerly, not wanting any possible piece of evidence to fall out. He thumbed gently through the contents, noting about seven hundred dollars in cash, a handwritten letter, and a few business cards bearing the name Bob Timson.

"Randall," he began sadly.

"No!" the man shouted, wresting his wrist from underneath Jacob's foot and rolling away. He was far more agile than Jacob expected, and was on his feet, running away down the street in an instant.

Jacob fumbled, taken aback. He had been all but blindsided by this revelation, and giving chase to a suspected murderer was almost the last thing on his mind at that moment. He paused for half a moment more, shook his head, and sprang into action. The billfold was quickly closed and tucked away safely into Jacob's own interior pocket. His revolver was unholstered and in his hand, and he set off.

"Get Lowry," he instructed to Holly as he darted away.

With more people out at this time of day, visiting neighbors or just taking the air, Jacob had to weave through a small crowd in his pursuit of Randall. The man had gotten enough of a head start that Jacob almost missed him turning the corner to a side street.

"Stop!" he shouted.

Couples he passed looked at him in surprise. Not one person stepped in to try to detain Randall in his escape. The owner of the Golden Saddle Saloon was beloved and well known in Tucson; Jacob was merely a bounty hunter, here one day and gone the next. Whose side did he expect them to choose?

But Jacob wasn't experienced with chasing outlaws for nothing. He was in far better shape than the saloon owner, and he lessened the distance between them with each stride. Around another corner, between two buildings, jumping over refuse and horse excrement in his chase.

"Stop, Randall! You're only making this worse."

Randall peeked behind him, then grabbed a nearby woman and shoved her toward his pursuer. Jacob caught her abruptly, before she could fall to the ground, and helped her regain her balance. Then he continued the hunt.

"I'm so sorry," he called over his shoulder.

Jacob still held his revolver while he ran. He was doing all he could to catch up to the probable murderer without having to shoot at him. Innocent bystanders were in every direction.

Randall turned another corner onto the

main street. As soon as Jacob realized where they were, he knew the man would be headed toward the Golden Saddle. He might have more weapons there, or barricade himself in his office, or even use his customers as human shields.

Jacob couldn't let him get that far.

He dug deep, reached into his reserves for a final burst of energy, and increased his sprinting speed.

He was gaining. Little by little, Randall Hall was getting closer.

With only thirty paces before the saloon door, Jacob felt himself within range of his target. He took one final near-leaping step, left his feet, and tackled Randall Hall around the waist.

The two men, tangled in a hostile embrace, crashed to the ground. A nearby woman screamed in surprise. Randall cursed and growled at Jacob, wriggling any direction he could to get free of the bounty hunter. But Jacob held on. He rolled them over, pinned Randall's body beneath him, and held the man's face into the dirt.

"You are under arrest, Randall Hall," he said finally.

The man didn't stop struggling. He didn't

seem to realize it was over, that he had been caught.

"You can't do this. You can't prove anything. Let me go!"

"Randall, stop. It's over. I don't want to have to hurt you."

The suspected murderer underneath him bucked like a bronco, trying to throw the larger man off of him, but Jacob held firm. Though he didn't have any rope or handcuffs on him— Jacob cursed himself for neglecting to be prepared—he could be creative. Still keeping his weight pressed into Randall, Jacob grabbed hold of the man's shirttail with both hands and ripped a long strip of fabric off the bottom of it.

"What the hell?" Randall exclaimed. "You're going to buy me a new shirt."

Jacob just shook his head, took hold of the man's left wrist, and bent his arm behind his back. With the fabric held tightly in his teeth, he did the same with the right wrist, until both arms were held together and he could tie them tightly using the strip of fabric as rope.

"You let me go!" Randall screamed. He sounded even more frantic, more out of control. In Randall's desperation, Jacob saw a glimpse of the violent man that had struck Holly earlier that morning.

With the man lying on his stomach on the ground, hands bound behind his back, Jacob had to help him to his feet. In spite of his very clear disadvantage, Randall didn't stop his protests or trying to break free of Jacob's hold. The bounty hunter had half a mind to knock him out, just to save himself the trouble of keeping him still.

A crowd had gathered; murmured questions sounded around them, and Jacob bowed his head politely to his audience. As he began to lead the still-protesting Randall back toward the sheriff's office, the whispers and grumbles sounded angrier. One large man with a red beard who Jacob didn't recognize didn't move to the side when Jacob reached him. He had to pull Randall around the stranger, pushing farther through the crowd.

"You got him!"

Jacob peered around several more people to spot Deputy Lowry striding toward him. The crowd started to thin, moving out of the way for the deputy and authority.

"This is an outrage!" Randall said.

"Oh, shut it," Lowry said. "Holly told me what you dropped."

"Wait—but I—"

"I said *quiet*. Now, Payne, let's get this man in a jail cell where he belongs."

With Randall finally under control, the finalization of their murder investigation went smoothly. By the next morning, Randall was booked and being held for the murder of Bob Timson. He had confessed the entire story. The case was on the circuit judge's docket for the following week.

Jacob took lunch at the San Xavier Cafe, eager for some peace from the three complaining inmates at the jail—as well as a possible chance at another of those sandwiches with fresh sliced peppers. With the murder solved, he'd need to be hitting the road soon, on the hunt for another outlaw, and he wasn't sure when he'd again get such a good meal.

"Hey there, Jacob," Bonnie said as he found a table. "I'm glad you came in today. I heard you had quite the Sunday afternoon. You're okay?"

"Yeah, everything worked out," Jacob said. "Just like it always does eventually." He smiled at her, appreciating the way her smile lit up the whole room.

"I know you probably shouldn't tell me," she said, lowering her voice to a whisper, "but did Randall Hall really kill that man? I can't hardly believe it. He always seemed like such a decent guy. And there were so many others that seemed much more likely to be murderers."

He looked around, but it was still early enough in the day that no one was near enough to overhear them.

"Sit down." He pulled out a chair for her and, once she was seated, pulled his own chair close to her.

"You're sure he did it?" she asked, leaning close to him.

Jacob was usually reticent to reveal details of his cases. But of all the people in the entire Arizona Territory who he wanted to protect, to comfort, to trust, and to shield, it was Bonnie Loft. He trusted her to keep the information to herself. He knew she would be strong, and would not want to be thought of as too delicate to handle these details.

"Well, I'm sure you understand we need to consider him innocent until his trial, but seeing as the man has confessed to all of this, I think we can presume this to be what happened.

"It seems that Randall Hall over-mortgaged the Golden Saddle Saloon and was hurting for cash. He claims he saw the kinds of funds Timson was throwing around and decided to see how he could get himself some of it.

Saturday night, he saw his opportunity and he took it."

Bonnie gasped. "Just like that? He just . . . he just *killed* him?"

"He did," Jacob said. "But what's worse is he tried to frame Holly Merritt for it."

"No!" She realized her exclamation had been too loud and leaned closer to Jacob. "How?"

"Clumsily," he admitted. "He told us she had handled the murder weapon. He told us she was poison and to watch out for her. He must have known she had a hefty savings and that would help point to her as well. But he didn't cover his tracks very well, and he hung on to the one piece of evidence we were certain had been stolen from the dead man."

"Why would he do such a thing?"

Jacob shook his head. "Pride, maybe. Or some misplaced feeling of victimhood. Seems Holly had told him she'd be leaving town. Maybe he wanted to punish her for leaving the saloon. Maybe he somehow thought if she was convicted of this crime, she'd have to stay. Maybe it was just the only thing he could think of to divert attention from himself. I don't know."

"Poor Holly," Bonnie murmured, looking away. "She was always so kind to me."

"She has a good heart. She doesn't deserve this."

"But she's leaving?"

Jacob nodded. "I talked to her last night. We had to interview her again, once all of Randall's machinations came to light. She is more than ready to get out of Tucson and start a new life in a bigger city. I think she's on the earliest stagecoach she could get on today."

"Do you think we'll ever see her again?"

Jacob shook his head. "I hope not. This has been her dream for a long time, and she's a good woman. I think this is exactly the right step for her. She deserves to be happy just as much as you and I do."

Bonnie's returning smile made Jacob think about all the ways he could make her happy, too.

FREE JACOB PAYNE STORY

Download this story for free—http:// atbutler.com/jp-free

Lonesome Trail

Before Jacob Payne arrived in the Arizona Territory, before he was a bounty hunter, before he learned how to survive in the desert, he had to travel west. Innocents in trouble, quirky characters and life-threatening peril are along every mile as he passed from Virginia through Texas to the desert of Arizona.

When Jacob comes across a family that has fallen victim to horse thieves, he can't just ride on and leave them to his fate. He's not yet a bounty hunter, but Jacob Payne can still hunt down the evil-doers. Tucson will be waiting for him once he brings these men to justice.

Sign-up to download this prequel story for free from my website: **http://atbutler.com/jp-free**

ALSO BY A.T. BUTLER

Jacob Payne, Bounty Hunter Series:

Trouble By Any Name

Danger in the Canyon

Justice for Jasper

Blood on the Mountain

Outlaw Country

Death By Grit

Desert Rage

Arizona Legacy

Fool's Demise

Silent Night

Courage on the Oregon Trail Series:

Westward Courage

Faithful Trail

Frontier Sisters

Unyielding Heart

Wild Promise

Fierce Dreams

Novels by A.T. Butler:

Hawke's Revenge

Loyalty's Price

————

Death by Grit, book six in the Jacob Payne series, is now available!!

Jacob Payne just wants to have a moment to breathe, go to church, and maybe court Bonnie Loft. But the U.S. Marshal in Tucson needs him. Seamus Maloney has just murdered seven innocent people when he held up their stagecoach, and the law in the Arizona Territory is not going to let him escape.

When Jacob follows Maloney's trail to the small town of Haven he is thwarted at every turn. Hindered by misinformation, incarceration, and injuries, the trail for the multiple murderer is going cold.

Will Jacob be able to stop the outlaw before his cruelty strikes again?

Get your copy now — atbutler.com/jp6

ABOUT THE AUTHOR

I grew up in the southwest—California Missions, snakes and constant threat of drought weaving the backdrop of my childhood.

But it wasn't until I moved to Texas a few years ago that the magic and mythology of the American West began to seep into my soul.

I'd love to write about Jacob Payne for a long time. ...

If you enjoyed this book, a review on your favorite retailer would be greatly appreciated.

- A

Outlaw Country is a work of fiction. Names, characters, places and incidents either are the product of the author's imagination or are used fictitiously. Any resemblance to actual persons living or dead, events or locales is entirely coincidental.

Copyright 2018 by A.T. Butler

Edited by Nerdy Wordsmith

Cover by Striking Book Covers

Print ISBN: 978-1-949153-08-8

All rights reserved.

No part of this publication may be reproduced, distributed, or transmitted in any form or by any means, including photocopying, recording or other electronic or mechanical methods, without the prior written permission of the publisher, except in the case of brief quotations embodied in critical reviews and certain other noncommercial uses permitted by copyright law.

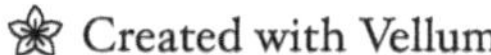 Created with Vellum

www.ingramcontent.com/pod-product-compliance
Lightning Source LLC
Chambersburg PA
CBHW021728190726
48288CB00009B/2956